MW01613988

THE SHOW JUDGE

Copyright © 2014 by Stuart R. Schwartz.

All rights reserved. No part of this publication may be reproduced, distributed, or transmitted in any form or by any means, including photocopying, recording, or other electronic or mechanical methods, without the prior written permission of the publisher, except in the case of brief quotations embodied in critical reviews and certain other noncommercial uses permitted by copyright law. For permission requests, write to the publisher, addressed "Attention: Permissions Coordinator," at the address below.

BookWhirl Publishing

PO Box 9031, Green Bay

WI 54308-9031, USA

www.bookwhirl.com

Ordering Information:

Quantity sales. Special discounts are available on quantity purchases by corporations, associations, and others. For details, contact the publisher at the address above.

Printed in the United States of America

Library of Congress Control Number:		2014910409
ISBN-13:	Paperback	978-1-61856-582-2
	Hardback	978-1-61856-586-0
	Pdf	978-1-61856-583-9
	ePub	978-1-61856-584-6
	Kindle	978-1-61856-585-3

Rev. date: 11/26/2014

Disclaimer

This publication is designed to provide accurate and personal experience information in regard to the subject matter covered. It is sold with the understanding that the author, contributors, publisher are not engaged in rendering counseling or other professional services. If counseling advice or other expert assistance is required, the services of a competent professional person should be sought out.

THE SHOW JUDGE

A Novel

By
Stuart R. Schwartz

Dedicated to the memory of
Am. Can. Champion Golden Kelby Dustan

Chapter One

The school's "dismissal" bell rings at 3:20 PM on a sunny spring afternoon at Truman High School in Gary, Indiana. The Senior Class is always allowed to leave the building first and the seniors rush to dominate their areas of the school yard where they engage in post-school banter. Each class has its own "neighborhood" in the school yard, and each neighborhood is represented by various cliques who established their boundaries early in the school year. Truman High is one of six public and private high schools in Gary and their students are known for their allegiance to the school. Rivalries are strong between the local schools, but Truman is known for its character. It isn't known for its academic prowess, and its sports teams were mediocre at best. But, there was an unexplained camaraderie amongst almost all of its students and they wear their colors strong.

Margaret Edwards is winding up her junior year. She seems quite animated as she exchanges quips with two friends beside a tree in the "juniors' neighborhood". Her long, golden hair sways from side to side as she waves her hands and laughs aloud. Margaret's two friends appear to be highly amused at what Margaret was sharing. Their laughter resonates throughout the "neighborhood". Margaret's younger brother Curtis, a sophomore, is heading home and easily recognizes his sister's repeated guffaws. His path home crosses through the junior's neighborhood, so he decides to approach Margaret.

Margaret greets him with a "Hi 'Curdles', heading home?"

"It's 'Curtis', 'Maggot'. Can I hang with you for a while? I'm not ready to go home yet."

"We're talking about boys Curtis and you aren't one of the ones we're discussing, so skedaddle. Just go home and do your homework."

"Bye 'Maggot'. See you at home."

The girls continue to giggle as Curtis leaves the scene. Curtis decides to stroll down one of the city streets on the way home from school. It is almost 4:00 PM and the sky is slightly overcast. At times Curtis skips, and then returns to a stroll. He passes a woman with a German Shepherd dog on a leash, obviously taking a "potty walk". She has a leash in one hand and a paper bag with paper towels in the other. As he passes, Curtis slows to a walk and turns to watch the woman go by. He decides to take his time getting home, so he passes the time by stopping by a small park and proceeds to plop his backside on to a bench. As he breezes through some school books, he quickly becomes bored, and then pulls out a comic book. Curtis ultimately arrives home and enters through the back door. His mother is in the kitchen doing some "prep work" for the evening dinner. His sister, Margaret, who beat him home, is sitting at the kitchen table reading *Seventeen Magazine*. Mom seems quite happy to see the kids at home from school.

"Hi Curtis."

"Hi Mom."

Margaret feels compelled to greet Curtis as well. "Hi 'Crude Ass'."

"Mom, why did you have to name me 'Curtis'? And she's not the only one that does that to me. Yesterday, Wendy called me 'Curtsie' in arithmetic class right in front of the teacher and everyone else for that matter. It caused a stir amongst some of my classmates, so I felt like a geek."

"Why do you have to worry about what other people think? Just ignore them, Curtis."

Margaret feels compelled to chime in, "Yeah 'Curdle', just ignore them."

Curtis has heard enough and decides to go for a walk. "Mom, I'm out of here for a while. I'll be back in time for dinner."

"Your Dad will be home from the Pharmacy at 5:00. We're eating at 5:30...be on time or we'll eat without you."

"Don't worry Mom, I wouldn't give 'Margaret, the Maggot' the satisfaction of gobbling my dinner. Sides, doesn't appear that there's much room left for anything else under those jeans."

Offended, Margaret screams, "MOM!!!!"

"It's about time the two of you thought about doing some growing up."

Curtis heads out the door and begins his brief journey to the junkyard, his favorite haunt. The junkyard is only about ten blocks from the house. It is a place where he can enjoy the solitude of this retreat as he can "hang there" without any outside annoyances. Curtis has few friends, by choice, and he finds solace with his alone time. When he arrives at the junkyard, it is eerily quiet. Looking around for any signs of life, he recognizes that he is indeed safely alone and seeks out a place to sit. An old bumper, seemingly dislocated from a vehicle many moons ago, rests alongside a pile of scrap metal. Curtis shuffles his way over to the bumper and plops himself on it as a temporary resting place. He peers into the sky and looks around at the relics of old vehicles, farm equipment, and various other scraps of metal from unidentifiable origins. Some are rusted out and others have remnants of paint on them. Suddenly, there is a sound from around the corner of an old Ford sedan. Slightly startled, he keeps looking in that direction. What immediately appears to be the nose of a ragged dog emerges from behind the Ford. The dog is more startled by Curtis than Curtis is by it. Slowly rising, Curtis moves carefully toward the spot where the dog was spotted. Even with his soft, tentative footsteps, the dog sees that Curtis is approaching and takes off like a shot.

"Here, doggie, doggie. I won't hurt you. Come here.................please."

Curtis chases the dog for a brief while and realizes that it is quite elusive and virtually uncatchable, so he heads back to the bumper, catches his breath, and eventually rises for the short journey back home. When he arrives home, he enters the house through the back door in time to see everyone assembling for dinner. Dinner conversation is normally animated in the Edwards household. Margaret and Curtis generally exchange barbs until asked to quiet down and their parents discuss anything that is new and exciting in Gary, Indiana, a ritual that is usually brief for obvious reasons. Curtis' Dad, Grayson Edwards, is a professional looking man in his 50's who works as a pharmacist at a privately owned local Mom & Pop drug store. As a pharmacist, Grayson hears all the scuttlebutt about town but, employing the use of his own personal filtering system, is careful to reveal only that which is "family friendly". Though the kids are somewhat more in tune with the more sensitive gossip than their parents, Grayson opts to share these episodes with only his wife at a venue other than the dinner table.

Grayson, curious about Curtis's whereabouts asks, "Take one of your walks again today, Curtis? And, by the way, where do you go? Nobody ever sees you. And what about your homework, son?"

Of course Margaret feels the need to chime in, "Obviously he isn't out chasing girls."

"Shut up, 'Mugsie'. And Dad, that's a load of questioning."

Mom, usually put off by the constant haranguing asks, "Can we ever stop this bickering? Can we eat? In peace?"

"We can if 'Curdle' stops calling me names."

"Who started the name calling, 'Mugster'?" asks Curtis. "Dad, I just like to walk. I go to different places and don't worry; they are all safe places to go. I can get my homework done after dinner. I finish it faster than most other kids. My report cards haven't been bad, right? Plus, it gives me time to reflect."

"Reflect son? That's an interesting emotion for a 15-year old."

"That's what I do, Dad."

During the course of dinner, without anyone noticing, Curtis picks out pieces of his meat loaf and stuffs them in a small "baggie" that he conveniently holds on his lap. He is determined to find the dog he saw at the junkyard earlier in the day. On the following day, Curtis leaves school and heads directly home. Upon reaching the house, he again enters through the rear door and walks directly into the kitchen where Mother is working on an apple pie. He is eager to return to the junkyard and try to befriend the dog he saw.

"Hi Mom, bye Mom, gotta run, see you for dinner."

"Where are you off to, Curtis? Oh, never mind, just be back here by 5:30, OK?"

"No prob Mom, see ya!"

Curtis walks into his room, throws his book bag onto his desk, reaches under the bed, pulls out his little baggie of leftover meatloaf, sticks it in his pocket, and heads out the door. His pace commences as a walk but eventually transitions into a trot as he heads for the junkyard where he arrives ten minutes later. He quietly takes his place on the bumper and sits patiently hoping that the stray dog will once again appear. After sitting for 15 minutes, he pulls out a comic book from his back pocket and begins to peruse the pages. Ten minutes into his reading, he hears a quiet rustle from the area where the Ford sedan is sitting. Looking over, he once again spots the ragged dog.

"Hey doggie. Come here boy....girl...whatever you are."

The dog, sensing that Curtis isn't as much as a threat as he appeared to be the day before, stands without running off, but securely holds his ground.

As the dog looks at Curtis with a curious, yet wary eye, Curtis has a chance to study its' features. Observing the recognizable protrusion from behind the rear of its lower body, Curtis determines that his soon to be new canine friend is a male. His coat is a ragged gray and obviously hadn't been groomed in a long time, if ever. His eyes are piercing and gray, almost like an Alaskan Husky, reminding Curtis of photos of this or similar breeds that he had seen in the past. Curtis notices that the dog does not take his eyes off of him. The dog's head is dropped lower than its torso almost to appear to be sending a message that he would prefer not to be approached. His legs were slightly bent at the knees which likely created a spring-board for him to bolt if necessary.

"It's OK doggie, I am not going to hurt you. I want to be your friend. Do you live in that Ford?"

The immediate response from the dog is a mere tilt of his head to the right. His ears prop up simultaneously with the tilt of its head as if to ask Curtis to repeat that question. It becomes obvious that the dog is not going to approach. Rising up very slowly, Curtis stands erect, and heads in the dog's direction with bait in hand. After two or three steps, the dog runs off. Judging from his gait, Curtis discerns that the dog appears to be slightly lame. Reaching into his plastic baggie, Curtis extracts three pieces of his "stash" and strategically creates a path that leads towards where he had been sitting. Curtis returns back to the bumper and sits and waits.

After fifteen minutes, the dog reappears and senses that there are remnants of food nearby. To Curtis, this appears to be the opening of a door to an interlude. The dog slowly moves towards the prize and, while never taking his eyes off of Curtis, cautiously picks off each of the three pieces of meatloaf. Recognizing that there will be no more, he dashes off back behind the Ford, only to step on an errant hubcap on the way. Curtis's only reaction was to mutter "Damn!!" The hubcap bears the word "Dodge" on it.

"That's going to be your name if I find you… 'Dodge' or maybe 'Dodger'. Nah, I'm going to call you 'Hubcap'. "Yes, 'Hubcap', I like that much better!"

Curtis does manage to arrive home just in time for dinner. Grayson Edwards is home from work already and the family is sitting around the dinner table. Trying not to be noticed, Margaret curiously peers over her extended fork at the uncharacteristically quiet Curtis. Curtis remains quiet, excuses himself, and heads to his room for homework and some pondering before retiring for the evening. As he leaves the table, the other Edwards's look at one another in a curious manner. Not a word is spoken.

The very next day, Curtis decides to feign ill and secures a pass to the Truman High nurse.

"May I help you, young man?"

"I'm sick."

Nurses deal with all types of bona fide illnesses and "pretendo" illnesses all day long. She takes a look at his hall pass, observes his name, and with a suspicious look on her face asks "What ails you, Mr. Edwards?"

"It's Curtis."

"Okay, what ails you, Curtis?"

"I think it was the tuna salad in the cafeteria for lunch that made me sick, yeh, the tuna salad. My stomach is upset. I feel like I want to barf."

"We don't use that word here in school, Mr. Edwards. The proper term is 'vomit'."

"Whatever. I am sick and I want to go home."

"Well, I'll have to call your Mother about this. She will have to come get you, ya know. Is she at home?"

"She should be."

As Mrs. Edward's car rumbles out of the high school parking lot, Curtis's Mom turns her head towards Curtis and with a quizzical look on her face asks him what this is all about. "Are you really sick? Or is this some kind of a ploy?"

"I'm not sick, Mom. I am sorry you had to drive out here to pick me up, but I just had to get out of the school. I have something to do Mom, but please believe me when I tell you that it isn't bad. It's actually a good thing but I can't tell you about it yet. I promise I'll tell you and Dad eventually. Look at it as if it is a project. And, I'll be home in time for dinner."

"I trust you son, but just be safe, ya hear?"

"Yup."

The ride home couldn't go quickly enough. Immediately upon arriving home, Curtis quickly retrieves the remainder of his meatloaf treats and heads straight to the junkyard. This time his step is more rapid than before, even breaking into a sprint. He seeks out his bumper and slowly takes a seat.

This time "Hubcap" appears much sooner. As if he expects that his new friend has something in store for him, Hubcap curiously stares directly at Curtis's outstretched hands. Curtis gets up slowly, empties a few treats into the palm of his right hand. Hubcap watches carefully without moving from behind the Ford sedan. Curtis moves very cautiously in his direction, treat-laden palm outstretched. He notices that Hubcap isn't going to budge, so halfway between the bumper and the Ford, he lays the treat down on the ground, keeping enough in his hand to lure his new four-legged friend closer.

Curtis slowly retreats to the bumper, walking backwards so as not to lose sight of Hubcap. As he is moving, he sees that Hubcap begins to limp towards the treat and quickly consumes it. Hubcap looks up as if wondering when the next treat will arrive. Curtis holds his ground, reaches out his hand, and watches as Hubcap slowly, cautiously moves in his direction.

"Come here, Hubcap....I'm your friend. That's why I am here. Don't be afraid. Please come, please... good puppy."

Hubcap approaches Curtis more proudly and takes a treat from his outstretched hand. His tail drops to the friendly and outstretched position and moves back and forth horizontally. Curtis identifies the motion as one of tentative delight.

"That-a-boy....want some more? Just stay here and I'll give you more. Don't move. I'm only going to reach into my pocket."

Hubcap, in his most obliging manner, patiently sits and waits for the next morsel. Curtis carefully reaches into his pocket, grabs the remaining pieces, and empties the remainder of his stash onto the ground. He gets up to see if Hubcap will follow him. As Curtis rises and heads for the gate to the junkyard, Hubcap turns around and heads in the opposite direction.

"Bye boy, see you tomorrow."

Curtis is up early and prepares his excursion to the junkyard. It is Saturday morning. The sky is a smoky gray and a light drizzle falls. The weather will not be a deterrent to the mission, so in his hand is a makeshift collar, a leash, and a baggie of newly purchased dog treats. Upon arriving at the junkyard, Curtis immediately notices that Hubcap is waiting by the bumper instead of beside the Ford sedan. The light rain had created an ever so slight muddy film on the surface of the ground and it became immediately obvious that Hubcap had taken an extended roll in it. Curtis walks over to him and sits by his side. Hubcap looks up at Curtis with a mournful eye. Curtis reaches into his pocket and extends a treat to Hubcap who instantaneously devours it.

"Gee Hubcap, you're hungry. I need to get you a good square meal."

This appears to be the best time to lure Hubcap to the makeshift collar and leash. He accomplishes the maneuver by having a dog treat in the same hand as the collar. Amazingly, as if he associates the new contraption with rations, Hubcap agrees to the collar and is totally prepared for the excursion.

The walk home was as painful for Curtis as it was for Hubcap. The limp had worsened, so Curtis picks up an agreeable Hubcap and carries him the remainder of the way home. Entering through the rear door, both Hubcap and Curtis look like they took a mud bath together. Curtis and his new friend are immediately greeted by Margaret.

"Yuck! Oh God, Curtis! Mom is going to kill you!!!!"

Sensing that he has met the enemy, Hubcap greets Margaret with all teeth bared, nose curled up, tailed tucked, back hairs standing on end, and a highly intimidating growl. Hubcap doesn't make it into the house.

"Get it out of here, Curtis. I mean it! NOW! Get it out! OH GOD!! Eeccccchhh!!!!"

"Margaret, cool your engines a second."

"I SAID OUT!!! NOW!!! AGGGGHHHHH!!!!"

Curtis and Hubcap retreat out of the door. They head towards the veterinary office of Dr. Vernon Holmstead. Curtis feels that the limp needs to be attended to and it may have had something to do with the dog's overall disposition. On the way to the vet, Curtis and Hubcap stop for a rest in the park. Curtis sits down on the bench, Hubcap attentively at his side. Hubcap, appearing to be apologizing, peers into the eyes of Curtis.

"Ya know boy, your limp and this park reminded me of something that happened when I was a little kid. Dad and I took walks through this very same park quite often. One time, we stopped and watched as two dogs, running alone in the park, played. Then one of the dogs mounted the other dog from behind and they were moving very slowly, panting, etc. I asked Dad what was going on and he told me that the dog on the back had hurt its' paw and the dog in the front was doing a 'good deed' by carrying him around on his back. Now that I am older, I realize that Dad was just plain bullshitting me. They were trying to make puppies. I'm just not sure why he didn't tell me that in the first place?!"

Chapter Two

Dr. Holmstead's office is only about a mile from the Edwards residence. The stand-alone building is old and small but had been painted with a fresh coat of light blue with white trim. There are four white stairs directly in front of the entrance with a small porch with benches for prospective clients who wished to wait outside. The waiting room is also small but large enough to accommodate the limited number of pets that the clinic would see in a day. Dr. Holmstead is advanced in his years but has the reputation of being kind, caring, and very effective at his craft. The office receptionist, named Anita, has also been there practically as long as Dr. Holmstead.

The waiting room is quite empty except for a woman in her early thirties' who is sitting quietly with her finely feathered dog sitting obediently at her side. She and Curtis exchange smiles while Hubcap shies away and squeezes close to Curtis's side. Anita, the receptionist looks up and while intently gazing at Hubcap speaks to Curtis.

"How may I help you?"

"Well, my dog seems to be a bit lame, and his eye runs."

"How long have you noticed the limp and the eye problem?"

"Well, uhm, let's see....uh, about a week. No, maybe a month."

"There's a big difference, young man, between a week and a month."

"Well, you see I really haven't had him that long."

"How old is he?"

"Not sure."

"Not sure. OK, how long have you had the dog?"

"Well, about an hour."

"An hour."

"Yup."

"Does he have a name?"

"Hubcap."

"Hubcap. And, who might I ask gave you Hubcap?"

"Nobody, I found him."

"You found him."

Curtis becomes visibly annoyed that the receptionist, Anita, feels compelled to repeat everything he says.

"Look. I like pets. I have had a few cats but never a dog. So, I hang out by the junkyard and I look for strays. This dog was hungry and lame, so I fed him. Now I want to see if he can get some attention from the vet."

"I see."

"You see." A touché seemed to be in order.

"Okay, have a seat and I'll see if we can squeeze you in."

Curtis is unsure about the "squeeze you in" remark as he and the other woman in the room are the only noticeable clients. "Thanks Ma'am."

A mild case of anxiety finds Curtis quite restless so he decides to engage the thirty-ish woman in conversation.

"Excuse me, ma'am, what breed of dog is that?"

"My dog?"

Curtis is bewildered by that response. She is the only other person in the room with a dog.

"Yes, ma'am. I was just interested in knowing because she is so beautiful."

"He."

"Sorry, He."

"It's a Golden Retriever."

"What's his name?"

"'EBA'. I know that sounds like an unusual name for a dog, but my Dad was a big fan of Abe Lincoln and knew all about his life and his Presidency. So, as a tribute to my Dad, I named him EBA, which is ABE backwards. I didn't think the dog would have appreciated being called ABE."

"Is EBA sick?" Upon hearing his name from a stranger, EBA's ear perk up, a doggie smile follows, and his tail begins swishing on the floor.

"No, he's just here for some annual shots."

Anita leans over the reception counter and speaks out to the woman. "The doctor is ready to see EBA now."

Curtis politely extends his "bye bye" greeting to the woman and EBA. Anita, the receptionist acknowledges that Curtis and Hubcap are still waiting.

"Just a few more minutes and Dr. Holmstead will be happy to take a look at Hubcap."

After ten minutes of waiting, Hubcap begins to whine. There is something about these new surroundings that he feels are less than appealing. The receptionist's eyebrows seem to raise and lower in unison with Hubcap's whines. The examination room door is about five feet to the left of the reception counter. And, after just a few more minutes, Dr. Holmstead peers out from behind the door.

"OK son, let's take a look at your friend."

Hubcap receives the full examination. Dr. Holmstead excuses Curtis and keeps Hubcap in the examination room. Curtis eagerly awaits the results in the examination room and finally Dr. Holmstead returns to speak with him.

"Son, we're going to keep your dog overnight and treat his eye. I believe his limp is due to an infection on his foot. He simply doesn't want to put any pressure on it. Anita will call you in the morning and let you know how he is doing."

Anita addresses Curtis as he re-entered the reception room. "Young man, before you leave, by what means would you like to pay today's charges?"

"By what means, ma'am?"

"Yes, how do you wish to pay for your dog's visit?"

"Oh, well, how much is the bill?"

"How much is the bill? Well, let's see. That's twelve dollars for the examination, five dollars for the anti-inflammatory medicine, four dollars for the blood and stool samples, and five dollars for his distemper and rabies shots. The grand total is, let me see, damn this pen, uhmmmmm...carry the one, which would be twenty-six dollars."

"Uhmmmm, I don't have the whole twenty-six dollars on me right now."

"You don't have the whole twenty-six dollars on you right now. Well, how much do you have on you right now?"

Digging into the pocket of his jeans, Curtis proclaims, "I'm afraid I only have seventy-five cents right now, ma'am."

Anita's eyebrows begin to contort. "When will you have the rest? It is customary for us to be paid for charges at the time the pet is seen by the doctor. We normally do not make exceptions."

"I'll ask my dad. He'll probably help me pay the bill. May I see Dr. Holmstead one more time before I leave? I need to ask him something."

"You need to ask him something? Why don't you just ask me, and I'll convey the message to him."

"Well, I want to work off my debt."

"You want to work off your debt. Doing what?"

"Whatever you need someone to do around here. I dunno. Clean the kennels, wash the pets, stack the dog food, anything."

"I'll talk to Dr. Holmstead about this issue when he is finished seeing patients. In the meantime, why don't you try to make some arrangements to pay your bill."

"Thank you. I will do that and I'll wait for your call."

A young boy is exposed to many emotions but coping with the issues surrounding these emotions are a challenge as they are usually new to a youngster. Curtis is no exception and he finds himself pondering how to address this new adventure with his family. The same night as his visit to the veterinarian, he finds himself watching some mindless TV show with

Mom and Dad after dinner. With so much on his mind, the TV show is merely a blip in his sights accompanied by some background noises. The sounds of his sister, giggling and bantering with a friend who is visiting, come from the top of the stairs from behind her bedroom door.

"Mom, Dad, I have something to tell you."

Curtis's Dad is the first to acknowledge him. "I assume this is about your excursions, son."

Curtis doesn't immediately respond but manages to wiggle himself deeper into his place on the couch. He realizes that perhaps he should have formally prepared his delivery, but lets it fly anyway. "Well, I have a love for animals, especially pet animals like dogs and cats. I never had a dog, but I have one now."

Mom & Dad both take their attention from the TV screen and look over at Curtis in a most quizzical manner. Curtis immediately feels as though he has been simultaneously lasered by four eyeballs.

"I've been going over to the junkyard just to have some time to myself and do my reflecting thing. I've told you that before. I just haven't told you where I've been going. Well, a few days ago, I found a stray dog in the junkyard. I named him Hubcap. He seemed to need a friend, and so did I. So, I got him to follow me but he needed a visit at the Vet, so I took him to Dr. Holmstead today. I couldn't pay for his bill, so I asked if I could work it off. I should hear from him soon."

It's Dad's turn to speak. "So you are 'reflecting' again, son? That's interesting. So, what do you plan to do with this dog once he is well?"

"I was hoping he could become a family pet."

Mom feels it is time for her to chime in. "Well we haven't even discussed this, Curtis."

"I was hoping that is what we could do now."

Mom is silent for a second, looks at the ceiling of the room, scratches the bottom of her chin, and suggests, "I think Margaret should be a part of this discussion. After all, she may have to be one to help take care of this dog."

"The dog's name is Hubcap, Mom, and no! Margaret will never agree to anything I want to do. And it's not just because of the dog, it's because she wants me to be miserable."

"Why, I don't believe that's true, Curtis." Mother moves towards the stairs and calls upstairs for Margaret. "Margaret!"

"What Mom?"

"Would you please come downstairs for just 5 minutes? Dad and I have something important to discuss with you."

Margaret leaves her friend behind and heads downstairs to see what Mother wants. "Margaret, Curtis wants a family pet and found a dog. It is at Dr. Holmstead's now and will be here tomorrow if we all agree."

Margaret does not hesitate to deliver her response. "Well I DON'T agree, especially if it's that mangy vicious dog that 'Crude-ass' had here this afternoon."

"He needed a bath 'Maggot', and he's getting one now, and he isn't vicious. He was scared, mainly because you scared him. Plus, his foot hurt and he was defending himself."

"I scared HIM Curtis??!! No, wrong!! You collectively scared the crap out of me! Then he freaked out. I say NO!!!"

Curtis's unrefined negotiating skills were immediately deployed into action, and almost instinctively suggested, "How about on a trial basis? If he doesn't work out, I'll find another home or I'll take him to the shelter. But I really believe he'll be fine! A one week trial. That's only fair."

Margaret sits thinking for a few minutes. "I'll agree provided that I won't have anything to do with him. No walking, no feeding, no petting, no washing, no nothing. And if he eats my homework, bites me or any of my friends, pees in my room, or anything that is as distasteful as the time you left a banana under my pillow to rot when I was away at Girl Scout Camp, then he's gone, got it??!!"

"Deal!...Mom, Dad???"

Mom, without hesitation answers. "Fine by me, but I tend to agree with Margaret."

The sound of the telephone ringing interrupts the family conversation. Grayson, sitting next to the end table where the phone rests, answers the call.

"It's for you, Curtis."

"Oh, Hi Dr. Holmstead."

Having listened attentively to what Dr. Holmstead had to say, Curtis responds, "You will??? Oh gee, thanks Dr. Holmstead. Monday afternoon, after school? Great, I'll be there."

Turning to his parents, "Mom, Dad, that was Dr. Holmstead. He's giving me a job in order to work off my debt, and he said that if I did a good job, he will keep me on after the debt is paid and pay me two-fifty and hour."

Grayson appears happy that this conversation is temporarily behind them, "That's good, Curtis. Just keep up your end of the deal, OK??"

"You got it, Dad."

Chapter Three

The new, sound, and neatly groomed Hubcap is back in his new home at the Edwards residence. The training commences. Housebreaking doesn't take long but the basic commands are not working. Curtis decides to head to the library to seek out a book on dog training. The Lake County Library is as old as any building Curtis has ever entered. He feared that if he walked up the stairs to the front door too heavily, his foot might fall through. Taking each step at a time, the creaky door is opened and an attractive elderly librarian, perhaps as old as the building itself, is smiling and beckoning his request. With all the confidence of knowing exactly what he seeks, Curtis approaches the counter.

"How may I help you today, young man?"

"I am trying to train my dog but I am not sure I am using the correct methods. I was wondering if there is any type of book that can help me teach him obedience and tricks, yah, tricks."

"Well, we haven't had much call for a book of dog training, but we do have a section on pets. Let's you and I meander over there and see what we can find. I'll need to go back to the librarian desk when we are finished but feel free to go through these racks and if you find something that you like, just bring it back to me and I'll check the book out for you."

"Okay, thanks ma'am."

The books in the section seemed a bit older than most and a thin layer of dust reveals that none

of them had been checked out in recent months, or
years for that matter. As the librarian had indicated,
the selection was indeed sparse but Curtis manages
to find two books on the principles of dog training.
He carefully pulls them out of the racks so as not
to disturb the older bindings and proceeds to check
them out as directed.

Curtis wastes no time returning home from the
library where he will begin his lessons on training
Hubcap. He zips through the back door and high-
tails it to the bedroom. Hubcap, almost keenly aware
that this excursion involves him, joins the race and
takes a place on the floor right alongside his new
master's outstretched body. Hubcap watches as
Curtis studies his books on dog training. In his dog
mind, he has not been able to determine that these
studies would be the guides of a better life for both.
A series of days follow wherein Curtis is diligently
working in his backyard with Hubcap, teaching him
all of the basics. Mutual delight is preempted by the
show of progress each day.

A few weeks pass and the Edwards family, sans
Margaret, is indulged in the living room watching TV.
Grayson becomes bored with what they are watching,
walks up to the TV, and manually begins changing
channels. He happens across a non-network station
that is broadcasting a dog show live from Chicago.

"Dad, wait, stop there."

"Curtis, your Mother and I are not interested in
watching a dog show."

"Yeah, but Hubcap and I are."

Mom decides to show her support, "It's OK
Grayson, there wasn't much else to see anyway and

I would just assume read my magazine." A recent edition of *Better Homes & Gardens* is sitting on the end table. Mom picks it up and slides it on to her lap. Curtis and Hubcap are fixated on the televised dog show. Hubcap lets out with a slight growl when he sees the dogs parading across the screen. Grayson half-heartedly watches and, having not finished reading the newspaper earlier, looks at the *Chicago Gazette* at the same time.

It was time to return the dog training books to the library. At the same time, the light bulb that was flashing between Curtis's ears prompted him to revisit the racks of books in the pets section to see if there is anything that related to dog shows. Upon entering, the librarian recognizes him immediately and greets him with an ear-to-ear smile.

"Hello again, young man. Is your dog trained now?"

"In fact, he is ma'am. I was wondering if you have any books on dog show training?"

"Hmmmm...well that might be a wee bit more difficult to find, but you know where the pet section is, so why not go take a look. Let me know if you need help."

Frustration mounts as Curtis peruses each volume in search of anything that smacked of dog show training. He finally surrenders and returns to the front desk. The librarian hasn't seemed to lose her smile as he approaches.

"I didn't have any luck, ma'am."

"I was afraid that might happen, so while you were looking, I took the liberty to locate the phone number of the National Kennel Association in New

York. They oversee the registration of dogs, and everything that has to do with their welfare. I called them and they gave me an address to where you can write. They publish a handbook that tells all of the rules of dog showing, and it even provides some pointers. Here's the address. Good luck!"

"Wow! Thanks a lot, ma'am."

Never losing her smile, "It is my pleasure."

Curtis breaks into a full sprint, hair blowing in the wind, and makes it home from the library in record time. He enters completely winded, but with enough energy to head to his room where he crafts a letter to the National Kennel Association.

When it is finished, Curtis quietly repeats what he wrote.

Dear National Kennel Association,

I am a 15 year old boy in Gary, Indiana, and I saw a dog show on television. I have a dog named Hubcap that I found in the junkyard. I have been training Hubcap and now I want to take him to a dog show so that he will have ribbons. It will make both of us proud. The librarian in our county library told me that you have a manual that you can send me that will tell me about dog shows. Please mail it to me at the address on the envelope so that I can get started.

Thank you.

Curtis Edwards

Each day, Curtis races home from school to check the mailbox in front of his house. For each day that there is no response, he becomes more despondent. He resigns himself to the fact that he would not hear from the Kennel Association. But, three weeks later, Curtis returns home from school and notices a manila envelope sitting on the kitchen table. It is addressed to him. Mom is standing in the kitchen when he arrives. She seems as eager to see Curtis's reaction as Curtis is to open the envelope.

"Curtis, this little package came for you today."

"Thanks, Mom."

Almost tripping on the stairs as he flies, he heads for his bedroom and tears open the package.

Curtis reads the letter out loud.

Dear Mr. Edwards,

Your letter was delivered to my desk so that I could address your inquiry. Included in this package you will find a pamphlet that is an overview of the National Kennel Association. The other pamphlet is a summary of dog showing principles and practices. I hope that these will meet your needs. On a personal note, the Association was formed to promote the health and welfare of registered breeds of dogs. Unless 'Hubcap' is a registered breed, he will not be eligible to compete in NKA sanctioned dog shows. But, please do not lose faith as there are dog shows all around that are organized just for fun. They oftentimes accept dogs that have no designated breed or registry. If you love dogs as

much as I think you do, you would have some
fun participating in such an event. I wish you
the very best of luck.

Sincerely,
Susan Mulvany, Associate Director

After digesting some of the larger, unfamiliar words in the letter, Curtis begins to pile through the contents. The dog showing pamphlet is laden with many photographs. They depict dogs of several different breeds in various shows. Under each photograph is a brief description of the type of dog and some dialogue about how they are handled by their handlers for the shows. Some of the breeds require different types of handling depending on the size and breed. The pamphlet will not be set down until Curtis is fully aware of how the showing procedures work. He is eager to try these out with Hubcap. The Edwards backyard becomes the training ground for Curtis and Hubcap. It is their own personal show ring, their practice field for the "big game" sans tents and judges. Each day, the two train on how to stand, move, and pose for a dog show. Progress is slow as Hubcap resists like a baby with a scratchy diaper, but there seems to be improvement daily. After several weeks, Curtis has Hubcap at the point where he will do a traditional dog show pose without coaxing and he will stay in that position. Hubcap has learned to not even move his head out of the correct position.

One Sunday morning as the family is enjoying breakfast, Curtis asks his Dad if he could take a gander at the *Chicago Gazette*. He has something to search.

"Curtis, the *Gazette* is on the end table next to the sofa. I hope you find what you are looking for."

The "events" section of the Chicago Gazette is vast, so Curtis would have to wade through a lot of unrelated outings before he would find what he was looking for. Craft shows, ethnic festivals, and rallies of all sorts dominated the pages. His quest to find a dog show in the Greater Chicago/Northern Indiana area reveals nothing. Slamming the newspaper down, he looks for and examines the phone book and finally finds a listing for Lake County Kennel Club. Knowing it is Sunday, he decides that he won't get anyone if he calls, so he waits until Monday after school to call.

"Thank you for calling Lake County Kennel Club, Marie speaking, how may I help you?"

"Hi, I'm Curtis Edwards and I am interesting in showing my dog."

Marie seems to wear a smile in her voice as she responds, "You are, are you? Well what breed of dog do you have?"

"Dunno."

"Then, why are you interested in showing your dog?"

As Hubcap stares at Curtis throughout the conversation, Curtis comes up with a manufactured but accurate response, "I saw it on TV. It looks like fun. My dog is trained. He would do well."

"What's your dog's kennel name?"

"Kennel name? Dunno. His name is Hubcap."

"So, am I to assume that 'Hubcap' is not registered with the NKA?"

"Ah, no. Never mind, it's OK"

"No, wait. I may be able to help you. Please repeat your name for me?"

"Curtis Edwards."

"Curtis, just because there isn't a place to show your dog through an NKA sanctioned show doesn't mean that there isn't a place to show him. There are several matches that are designed for people like you who want to show their dogs. And, in most cases, the dogs don't have the credentials to go to an NKA show. These are generally called 'fun matches'. In fact, there is a company that publishes a list of all upcoming fun matches. If you wait a minute, I can get their address and telephone number for you."

"OK, I'll wait." A pad and pencil happen to be directly across from where Curtis is sitting, so he lays down the receiver and makes a quick grab for them.

"OK, Curtis, the address is: Match Show Guide, P.O. Box 9998, Denver, Colorado. The telephone number is: (303) 555-9990."

"Thank you very much ma'am. I'll call them right now."

"You're welcome. It was my pleasure. Good luck, Curtis. Goodbye now."

A woman answers the phone on the first ring. "Good afternoon, this is Ellen."

"I want to receive the Match Show Guide."

"That's not a problem. Just send $4.00 to us at our address. Please be sure to include your name and address and we will send you the Guide for one year."

"I have your address and I'll do it today. Thank you."

"Thank you. Good bye then."

The Match Show Guide arrives on the following Friday. To Curtis's delight, there are several fun matches from which to choose. In some cases, there are as many as five or six on each weekend within 100 miles of home. On the very next day, Curtis, his Dad, and Hubcap, who is riding in the back seat, are in the car driving down the Indiana Toll Road towards South Bend.

"Son, I'm not sure how you talked me into driving you to South Bend."

"Dad, you know it's something I really want to do. Sides, what was more important? Cutting the grass? Doing all of those things around the house that Mom has on a list? And Dad, I think you'll have fun too."

With a sly chuckle, Grayson retorts, "Well, you did save me from the chores, son."

Finally pulling into a small park, they mutually agree that they have arrived at the right place. They see a few tents and a lot of people milling around with their dogs. The dogs are of all ages from small puppies to grown older dogs. Most of them appear to be "known" breeds. The day is clear, and the excitement of participating in his first fun match overwhelms Curtis with joy. His ear to ear grin tells Grayson that he is doing the right thing with his son.

"Dad, there sure are some fancy looking dogs here. I don't know if Hubcap has a chance."

"Ya never know until you try. There's a sign over by that desk that says 'registration'. Let's see what we have to do to get Hubcap registered."

The "registration desk" is a makeshift table with a paper cover held down by a rock on each corner. There are two folding chairs on the other side of the table. On the table are a few clipboards with pens attached by strings. It is likely assumed that pens at dog shows tend to disappear with the same frequency as they do in banks. A man and a woman occupy each of the chairs. Each has a serious, authoritative look on their face. For Grayson and Curtis, this encounter was going to be less than serious business. There is a small line of people waiting to register, each with dog in hand. Each of the dogs seemed well groomed and equally well behaved. Hubcap wasn't sure what to make of it all, but stands quietly, yet valiantly, awaiting directions from his master. Finally Curtis and Grayson are the next in line to register.

"Good morning. We're here to register my son's dog for the show."

The woman registrar is looking at Hubcap very oddly and with skepticism in her eyes. Instinctively, Hubcap looks straight into her eyes and tilts his head as if he knows she is looking at him. "There is a class for dogs that are mixed breeds. Have you shown the dog before?"

Curtis hesitated a bit as if to decide whether to provide a straight answer, or not, then, "Uhmmmm, No."

"Then you may want to enter him in the novice class. Just complete this brief form and that will be

$2.00 for the entry. Ring number eight is where the mixed breed novices will be shown."

Upon arrival at ring number eight, Curtis and Grayson notice that the other dogs are already getting set to enter the ring.

"Son, there are some very well behaved, well groomed dogs getting into that ring. Many of them seem to have handlers that are experienced. You sure you want to do this?"

"Dad, I know what I am doing. Hubcap and I have been practicing this for weeks."

As he enters the ring with Hubcap, Curtis encounters a few giggles, many of which are directed at him. He appears not to be intimidated at all. He has decided that his confidence in what he was about to do would outlast any element of anxiety associated with this little venture. There are eight dogs in the ring. They line up, each with a handler on the other end of their lead. The judge, a woman in her 40's, begins to look at each dog in the line as she stands at a short distance from where the handlers are working. When her eyes fall on Hubcap, she raises an eyebrow with a slight, smirky smile. She asks for the participants to take their dogs around the ring. With a leash in hand, the front handler breaks into a light trot and her dog diligently follows alongside. They all circle the ring twice and the judge raises her hand asking them to stop. She then asks the first participant to bring her dog by her side and with a "stop sign" gesture and asks the others to wait their turn. One by one, each dog is set by its handler to stand in a pose position while the judge examines the contestant with her eyes accompanied by a complete examination with her hands. Curtis winces as he wonders how Hubcap will respond to a judge's hands embracing his genitals. It becomes Hubcap's turn to face the judge.

Barking out his rehearsed command, Curtis shouts, "Hubcap, STAND!"

With no leash, and no bait, Hubcap launches himself into a perfect stand position. The judge does not say anything but has the "OH MY" look on her face. She runs her fingers up and down Hubcap's mouth, looking at his teeth, touching his face, under his chest, through his back, along his tail, and finally goes for the genital sack. Hubcap turns around, takes an admiringly look at the fondler, and does an uncharacteristic doggie smile. Hubcap's examination is complete and the dogs are asked to return to their places. All handlers are asked to take their dogs around the ring one more time and return to their places. The judge examines them one last time and awards the ribbons. Hubcap receives a third place ribbon.

As Curtis heads for the ring exit, the judge calls out to him. "Son, may I speak with you for a moment before you leave?"

"Sure!"

"Your dog doesn't stack up with the others as far as conformation and grooming are concerned. But I awarded you a ribbon today for another reason. Your handling abilities, though unorthodox, were very impressive. You had that dog doing everything it was supposed to do, basically with a simple oral command. You hardly touched him. I am sure you have a special relationship with your dog, but, quite honestly, in all of my years, I haven't seen anything like this. I am also a dog show handler. I only judge in these types of 'Fun Matches', but I can see that you have a keen talent. So, I just wanted to tell you to keep it up, don't quit, and you can do very well at this."

"Well, thank you, ma'am. I will. I will."

It was a joyful journey back to Gary from South Bend. With pride in his eyes, Grayson compliments Curtis on what he accomplished in the ring. "Good job, Curtis. I am proud of you! Out of curiosity, what did that judge say to you?"

"She said that I have a special talent and not to quit doing this."

Chapter Four

Two weeks later, Curtis and Grayson are in the car again, heading to Naperville, Illinois for another Match Show. Hubcap is diligently sitting in the back seat looking out of the window, taking in the scenery. There is an occasional bark or soft growl when he spots any other type of animal, small or large. Grayson seems to be enjoying these excursions as much as Curtis and Hubcap. It gets him away from the house and his chores while enjoying the fact that his son is having the time of his life.

On this particular occasion, there are nine other dogs in the ring with Hubcap. Knowing what to expect this time, Curtis watches intently as the judge goes through all of the usual machinations and awards Hubcap and Curtis a 2nd place ribbon for all of the same reasons. The next show, one week later is in Janesville, Wisconsin. Curtis is once again in the ring with several other dogs. This time Hubcap wins. Curtis and Hubcap embrace one another. As Curtis and Hubcap are leaving the ring, they are approached by a man and his daughter. The man is of medium build, distinguished looking, and about aged forty. His daughter appears to be in her teens.

"Young man, may I speak with you briefly?"

Curtis is still "on his high" from the win and is ready to talk to the man on the moon if he should so appear. "Sure."

"My name is Kenneth Arden and this is my daughter Joan. We live in Delafield, not far from here."

"I'm Curtis, and this is my dog, Hubcap."

"Nice to meet you. Well Curtis, Joan and I saw what you did in there with your dog and we thought that you must have some magic touch with show dogs or something."

"Nah, Hubcap and I are good friends and he just does what I ask."

"But, I am sure you took a lot of time to train him."

The daughter, Joan, sets aside the formalities and decides to get right to the point. "Will you train and show my dog for me?"

"I would but I can't. But thanks for asking me."

Joan wasn't prepared to take "no" for an answer. "'Can't' or 'don't' want to??!!"

"I can't. I go to school and I work at the veterinary office part time. We live far from here."

The dad, Kenneth, seeing how much Joan is intent on making this interlude a positive one for her suggests, "We would be happy to leave our dog with you for a few weeks while you train him, and of course we would pay all of the expenses, and pay you too."

"Can I have some time to think about it? I'd have to talk to my Mom and Dad about this. What kind of dog?"

Joan jumps back into the conversation. "He's a Standard Poodle."

Curtis looks at both of them and hesitates for a moment or two before he replies. "Why don't you give me your telephone number and I'll give you mine and that way I can call you if I decide to do it, okay?"

Kenneth does not want to leave with a disappointed daughter. "Sounds good, but you will seriously consider it, won't you?"

"Sure, I will. What's his name?"

Joan proudly blurts out, "Mountainview's Hardy Aurelius, but we call him Rex."

"Okay, I'll call you. Bye."

Simultaneously, father and daughter extend their farewells too, "Bye!!"

There was nothing unusual about the ride back to Gary, Indiana. The car was quiet. The car radio was tuned in to some soft, classical music. Hubcap was sound asleep in the back seat with the first place ribbon draped around his neck. Curtis had tried to remove it before boarding the car, but Hubcap knowingly refused to let Curtis grab it. He had earned it, it was his now, and nobody was going to remove it. The silence was finally broken with Grayson inquiring, "Son, who were those people with whom you were talking?"

"Some people that want me to train and show their dog for them."

"What did you tell them?"

"I told them I would think about it and call them."

"How would you do that, son? They probably live far from Gary."

"I know. That's why I've got to figure it out."

At dinner two days later, Curtis reveals his wishes. He directs his comment to Grayson. He knows that his Dad is keenly aware of his enthusiasm and expects a positive response.

"Dad, I think I want to try this."

"Try what, son?"

"Train and show those people's dog."

Mom is only peripherally aware of Curtis's new hobby. "What are you talking about, Curtis?"

And, of course, what would the conversation be without Margaret's two cents? "There he goes again. He's flaking out, Mother."

"I am not, Maggot! Dad knows what I am talking about. You do the stuff you wanna do, why can't I? Just shuddup, Okay?" Too busy eating and pondering whatever she may have had on her mind through her unusual silence prior to Curtis's remark, Margaret declines to retort.

But Grayson shows interest and sets up Curtis for a good answer hoping to placate Mom and Margaret. By referring back to their private conversation in the car a few days earlier, he asks, "How would you do this, son? They live so far away."

"I figured it all out, Dad. I already talked to Dr. Holmstead about it. See, these people would pay for their dog to stay here. Dr. Holmstead will board him for the amount of time it will take me to train him. I'll spend an hour each day working with him. It won't interfere with my work or my homework. And, they are going to pay me for it. I want to do this, Dad, Mom."

"OK, son. I believe your Mom and I would agree. But, I also think you should tell this family that it would be on a trial basis only and that if it isn't working out they would have to come down here and pick up their dog. Deal?"

With a broad smile, "Deal!!"

Joan Arden answers the telephone on the very first ring. "Hello?"

"Hi, this is Curtis Edwards in Gary. I promised to call you."

"Hi Curtis, it's Joan. What did you decide?"

"I'll do it."

As he waits for Joan's reaction, he can hear her yelling across a room. "Dad, it's that boy, Curtis, from the Fun Match. He said he'll do it. Yes!! Curtis, are you still there?"

"I am."

"We can bring Rex to you this weekend. Will that work?"

"Uhmmm, sure."

A late model Mercedes Benz pulls into the Edwards driveway at ten o'clock on Saturday morning. Rex is the first one out of the car and runs directly over to Curtis who has been diligently standing at the front door stoop awaiting their arrival. Both Kenneth and Joan Arden appear surprised that Rex immediately sought out Curtis, adding strength to the theory that dogs do indeed know "dog people" when they see (or sniff) them.

Joan greets Curtis with a hug and assures him, "Rex is my dog and my companion. Please take good care of him."

"Of course I will. I'll keep in touch with you and let you know how he is doing."

Shortly after Kenneth and Joan drive off, Curtis and his new pal Rex prepare to head over to Dr.

Holmstead's office. Hubcap watches intently from a front window and begins to whine. The whining continues and transitions to a howl which is a new phenomenon for Hubcap. Curtis relents, Hubcap and Rex do their obligatory butt-sniffing, and off they go to the vet. Anita, "the repeater", is at the reception desk adorned in her "casual Saturday" attire which includes jeans and a long sleeved T-shirt bearing a picture of a Doberman on the front of it.

"Anita, this is the dog I told you and Dr. Holmstead about. He'll be staying here a while. I am going to train him to be a star. "

"Pretty poodle. Sure Curtis, fine."

Each day, immediately after school Curtis walks to Dr. Holmstead's office. He has his vet chores to complete, and then takes Rex outside for training. This goes on daily for a few weeks. Rex is extremely cooperative and Curtis is enjoying the fact that there has been huge progress.

A call to the Ardens is in order, and once again Joan answers on the very first ring causing Curtis to wonder if she actually sits by the phone while at home.

"Is this Joan?"

"Yes, is this Curtis?"

"Yes. I am sorry I didn't call you sooner. Everything is fine with Rex. He's doing real well. He's quite intelligent and responds nicely to all of his training. He's going to work out great."

"We weren't worried, Curtis." We knew he was in good hands."

"Joan?"

"Yes?"

"I found a dog show, a real one, not a Fun Match, that they're having near Chicago in three weeks. Tomorrow is the last day I can enter Rex. Would it be OK? The entry fee is $15.00 but you can pay me back later. I won't charge you anything for showing him."

"I'll check with my Dad, but I'm sure it'll be OK. But, Dad will want to pay you."

"He can buy me a hotdog and a pop. I'll like mustard and relish on the hot dog. A Coke will do me fine too, but not that stuff without the sugar."

Noticeably chuckling, "I'll call you back later Curtis, OK?"

"That's fine."

Almost an hour to the second, the phone rings at the Edwards home. Curtis, eagerly awaiting a call back from Joan, answers on the first ring. "Hello???"

"Hi Curtis, It's Joan. Dad said fine. Just give us the date and time and we'll be there. I really miss Rex though. Can we pick him up sooner?"

"Yeah, I guess, but I will need him before the show to practice some more, okay?"

"Maybe we can meet half way. Dad doesn't mind driving me."

"Sounds good, Joan, bye."

The Ardens retrieve Rex the next day but return him to Curtis a few days before the big show in Chicago. Curtis spends as much time as possible working with Rex and reaches the point where he feels totally prepared for his and Rex's first big event, a sanctioned NKA dog show. The Greater Chicago Show Grounds are immense to the point that it is somewhat intimidating. Grayson, without acknowledging his emotions to Curtis, is also intimidated by what he sees and just hopes that Curtis will work through any anxiety and do his job.

"Holy shit, Dad! This is HUGE!!!"

"Watch your language son, and hey, it's the same thing as the Fun Matches, just a little bigger. Just relax, it'll be fine. Let's walk around and look for the Ardens. The Standard Poodles don't come on for a while."

"K!"

It didn't take long for the Ardens to spot Curtis, Grayson, and Rex among the crowds of mankind and canines. Rex is perfectly groomed and very happy to see his owners. They reunite.

Joan, holding Rex in her arms, asks "Curtis, how did you get Rex to look so good?"

"Well, Dr. Holmstead has a groomer that comes in once a week. I showed her the picture of the breed standard from the National Kennel Association. So, she groomed Rex based on what she saw. I was happy that she did a nice job with him."

"Are you nervous, Curtis?"

"Yah, a little, but we'll be OK. We're going against other 'Open Dogs', so at least there won't be any champions to go against."

The time comes for Standard Poodles to be up and Curtis, after awaiting the arrival of some of the other participants, enters the show ring with Rex. There are 18 dogs in the "Open Dog"class. The judge enters the ring and proceeds to go through all of the maneuvers in examining each dog. Curtis has Rex trained beautifully. All eyes are on Rex and the young and inexperienced "kid" who has the guts to get in there with him. Curtis can tell that the ring is laden with expert handlers. The judge's final request is that the handlers "take their dogs around". The judge motions them to stop and then moves Rex and Curtis to the front of the line. Curtis, in a bold and normally unorthodox move, takes off Rex's leash and asks him to "stand". Rex responds by spreading his legs a perfect distance apart and holding his head up high. The judge points to Rex as a winner. Following are screams of joy from the corner of the show ring.

Joan, almost breathless screams out loud. "Oh My God!!!!!!!!!!!!! Oh My God!!!!!!!!!! I can't believe it!!!! Oh My God!!!!!!!!!"

Though the lightning bolts of high emotion are running through every inch of Curtis's body, he has managed to hold on to his composure. "Oh, I was nervous, but when I saw that Rex wasn't, it was easy going from then on." As is often customary, several dog owners and handlers approach Curtis and congratulate him.

Grayson is ready to leave for home. He is not eager to break the strand of emotion but suggests, "Curtis and I have a long ride home, so we're going to 'hit the road'. I am sure we'll be in touch."

Kenneth understands and thanks Curtis with a strong handshake and a huge admiring smile. He hands Curtis an envelope. "Put this in your pocket and we'll be in touch." With all of the goodbyes behind them, Rex turns around to look at Curtis, almost curiously wondering why he isn't going back with him. The car ride back to Gary was quiet. About thirty minutes into the ride, Curtis reaches into his pocket and removes the envelope that Kenneth handed him. In it is three hundred dollars in cash.

"Dad, Holy shitenbarger! He paid me three hundred dollars!"

"You're joking!"

"No, look....three one hundred dollar bills."

A few days pass and while Curtis is busy finishing up some homework, he can hear the phone ring and his Mom pick it up.

"Curtis, it's for you."

"Who is it Mom? I'm doing homework. I'm at an important point here."

"I don't know, Curtis. Just pick up the phone, OK?"

"Okay, okay, give me a sec."

The phone extension outside Curtis's room is handy and he slowly strolls over and picks up the line.

"Hello?"

"Hello Curtis, my name is Barbara Sylvan. I got your name from the Ardens in Delafield, Wisconsin. I hope you don't mind that I am calling you."

"Course not."

"Well, I have a show dog, Curtis. Actually she's only been shown a few times, but she hasn't done much. She's a German Short-haired Pointer from a well-known breeder. She's pretty and has good conformation, but she doesn't show well. It's almost as if she's totally disinterested. I was wondering if you would like to train her and show her."

"Wow, don't know Ma'am. I have school, my own dog, and the Arden's dog, Rex."

"Well, if you can show her, her name's Mimi by the way, I'll pay you forty dollars for each time you show her plus your fee for training her."

"Where do you live Ms. Sylvan? And, can I have your phone number?"

"You can call me Barbara, and I live in Delafield also. And, my phone number is 555.8859. Curtis, please consider it. The Ardens said that they think you are a genius with dogs. Mimi needs someone who is good and who cares."

Not long after, a late model station wagon pulls up to the Edwards' house in Gary. Curtis stands at the front door when she pulls up. Out of the car steps a beautiful, elegant woman in her early 40's with a spotted sleek German Shorthaired Pointer.

"Hi, I'm Barbara. Are you Curtis?"

"I am. Nice dog. It's Mimi?"

"Yes, think you can train her?"

"If she's willing to learn, she will do just fine ma'am."

"I need to get back, Curtis." Didn't realize it was such a long drive. Driving through Chicago is a pain. Here's two hundred dollars to get started."

"Ma'am, I mean Barbara, don't give me any money now. Let's see how Mimi does and you can give me some money later."

"OK, but it is really worth a lot to us to have her do well. We don't have kids, so she's our little girl."

"She'll be staying at the vet's office, but she will get excellent care. Don't worry about her. She'll be fine. I'll keep in touch with you. Thank you, ma'am."

Two weeks later, Curtis calls Barbara with an update.

"Barbara, this is Curtis in Gary."

"Hi there Curtis. How's my Mimi?"

"She's doing great ma'am. Very nice girl."

"When will I see her again?"

"Well Barbara, that's what I wanted to talk to you about. There's a dog show, a pretty good one, in South Bend across from the Notre Dame University campus in a few weeks. It's on a Saturday and I would like to show Mimi. I am not sure of the competition yet, but I think she'll be ready. I also want to show the Arden's dog the same day, but I haven't spoken to them as yet. What do you think?"

"That would be fine, Curtis. I'll speak with the Ardens. Maybe we could ride together. They're friends of mine."

"That would be great. Thank you."

Barbara has agreed to allow Curtis to show Mimi at South Bend, so two weeks later Curtis is there with his dad Grayson, Rex, and Mimi.

As if Curtis has had this on his mind for some time, he poses a question to Grayson. "Dad, I am going to need to get equipped for these shows if I am going to continue to do this."

"What do you mean by 'equipped', son?"

"Dad, I'll need some crates for the dogs and a grooming table. Oh, and some grooming equipment too. Look around Dad, all of these other handlers have that all that stuff here. Hey, here comes Barbara, and the Ardens are with her. Wow, they sure got dressed up in their 'Sunday best' for a dog show. I guess I'm glad I wore this 'ole tie that mom makes me wear to church."

"Is that goin' to help you win, son?"

"Dunno, I'll take any help I can get."

Curtis makes his return to the show ring once again with Rex in tow. To everybody's surprise, Rex wins the open Standard Poodle class for the second straight time. Rex is in the ring awaiting his ribbon with the other winning dogs. A famous handler, Quinn Towler, obviously annoyed that such a young kid should have emerged as the winner of the "Winners Dog" class is in front of him also waiting to be photographed. Quinn is known as an arrogant, over-confident handler who is well known on the circuit. He commands a high fee and is highly respected for his dog handling abilities despite his demeanor. He is holding the Champion, a bitch. Curtis and Rex are a little too close to Quinn Towler for his liking.

"Having seen enough, Quinn 'barks' out at Curtis. "Hey, kid! Mind getting your dog's nose out of my dog's butt?"

Only a few seconds pass before Curtis decides that he won't be intimidated by Quinn. If he was going to play this game, he would do it like everyone else, or not do it at all.

"Uhmmm..how about getting your dog's ass out of my dog's face??!!"

"What are you kid? Some kind of a young wise ass?"

"You started it, mister. My dog is right where he is supposed to be. You backed into him."

"Why don't you just shut up kid and learn show ring etiquette."

"I know etiquette, mister. And, speaking of heads and asses, why don't you pull your head out of your ass???"

"You haven't heard or seen the last of me, you little piece of shit."

Another handler, Eve, also waiting for the photographer decides it is time to jump into the fray. "Quinn, leave the kid alone. He's just a kid."

"He's a wise ass kid, Eve, who doesn't belong in the ring."

"Quinn, you're just pissed because he's a little unknown kid with a few wins under his belt."

All depart the ring with snarls on their faces. The day turned out to be a doggie bonanza for Curtis as he scores a blue ribbon for Mimi in the German Short-haired Pointer ring. An ecstatic Barbara was the first to embrace him.

"That was fantastic, Curtis. You are everything the Ardens said you would be. I am so proud and thankful. Well, we're going to head back towards Milwaukee. We've got a bit of a trip ahead of us. What do I owe you, Curtis?"

"Oh, I dunno. I guess Fifty dollars is OK."

"Surely that isn't enough for your troubles Curtis. Here's an envelope for you. Keep in touch with me, OK?"

"Sure, Okay."

The Ardens are leaving at the same time. Ken makes it a point to tell Curtis that they would see him again soon. He too handed Curtis an envelope which he promptly stuffed into his pocket. Curtis and Grayson head towards the show grounds exits only to be stopped by a few more prospective clients.

A series of chats and an exchange of telephone numbers interrupted their plan for departure but neither seemed to mind the attention. There were no dogs to take care of since Rex and Mimi left with their owners. On the ride back to Gary, Curtis once again inspected his stash.

"Holy shitukas, Dad!!"

"What's that son? And the language? Shitukas?"

"Dad, yeah sorry, BUT, the Ardens gave me another hundred bucks, and Barbara gave me two hundred fifty. That's six hundred and fifty dollars in a month just for two dogs. That's more money than I ever made anywhere."

"That's VERY good son, but don't let it get to your head, OK?"

"Okay, okay, but crazy wow! Awesome wow!"

Chapter Five

Curtis's new bicycle shines brighter than a highly polished diamond. He has been proudly riding around the neighborhood showing it off and enjoying his first new ride in a long time. The feeling of having earned it himself creates a feeling of pride, a feeling that introduces an elevated spirit into his repertoire of emotions. As he approaches home, he waves to a neighbor and pulls into his driveway. In the basket in front of it is a wrapped gift for Margaret.

After dinner, the usual family tradition is to sit around in the family room absorbing any interesting television program that might be available to watch. The choices were limited, but it was something to do. This evening, all were present including Hubcap who is firmly planted at Curtis's side. The current TV show, a mindless game show, is boring and Curtis decides to give Margaret her gift.

"Hey, Maggot, this is for you."

"What's the present all about, Crude-ass?"

"Dunno. Just wanted to get you something. I got myself a new bike."

"Nobody just gets someone something unless there is a motive."

"What's a 'motive'?"

"A good reason Curtis, a reason. You must have a reason to do this unless it's some sort of a bribe."

"Well, I do have an idea. But it has nothing to do with the present. I just wanted to get you something. It helps me to celebrate my recent success."

"That's quite nice, Curtsie, but shit, can't hardly wait to hear about this idea of yours."

Mom, who seems to be ultra-sensitive about naughty language, jumps into the fray, "Margaret!!"

"Mom, 'Shit'!" is not considered a bad word. Everybody uses it except for on TV, so chill." Margaret opens the package to find a beautiful gold locket with a picture of Curtis and Hubcap inside the locket. "Oh my Lord!!! This is beautiful. Curtis, that was sooooo nice!!!"

"I thought you would like that. Get this Margaret....I am liking this dog showing stuff. I have already won and these people are paying me good money. I have a way with dogs and I can make them win. My point is that I can do more if I can get some help from you. Dad is already helping me by taking me all over the place. Dr. Holmstead lets me keep the dogs at his office while I train them. All I need is for you to help me and I'll share the money with you."

"You'll share it? Fifty – Fifty???"

"Depends."

"Depends? On what?"

"On how much you help me."

"Help you do what, Curtis?"

"OK, you have to learn how to groom. You will groom the dogs. You will be getting them ready for the shows. And when I am ready to go into the ring with the dog, you will bring the dog to me, then return the dog and watch over it while I move onto the next ring. And, Dad, you'll have to get a van to put the crates in. I'll pay it off from my money. It can be mine when I am old enough to drive. It doesn't have to be new. I can either borrow the crates from Dr. Holmstead or ask the dog owners to buy them."

"Curtis, I don't want to be washing any dogs."

"Grooming, Maggot, grooming. Washing is just a part of it. You can learn easily."

Grayson is listening intently to the exchange and suggests, "There are a lot of things to consider here, son. I am not sure about buying a van and what about school? I am concerned about your grades and Margaret's too. And will you have enough time to do all of this?"

"We'll have enough time, Dad. Trust me on this one. My grades will be fine too."

Margaret seems a bit more interested. "How much, Curtis? What's my take?"

"Twenty-five percent."

"No Curtis, fifty percent"

"Okay, I'll tell you what Margaret...I'll give you one-third. That's my final offer."

"Ok, that's a deal!"

"Dad, did you hear that?? We have a deal! It's a deal! Dad???"

It didn't take long for Grayson and Curtis to close the deal on a van at a local dealership and drive off. The van is a bright red, air conditioned, with side panels and vents on the top. It is large enough to seat at least four people and room in the back for six large dog crates and four small ones.

Meanwhile, Margaret has been spending ample time at Dr. Holmstead's with Curtis and the Groomer, Mary Holden. Curtis had already explained to Mary that Margaret needed to be well-versed in breeding practically any breed. Mary obliges by providing

Margaret with a book of all the breeds. The book also contains descriptions of the breed standards for each type of dog.

Margaret's anxiety is quite obvious as her patented look of frustration was seeping out from behind the locks of hair that careened across her face. "I'm not sure I can do this, Curtis."

"Of course you can, Margaret. You cut your friends' hair, don't you."

"My friends aren't dogs, Curtis! They don't move around and pant in my face when I trim their hair either."

Curtis finds this response somewhat amusing, and with a sly chuckle, "Yeah, right, okay then, let's practice on one of the boarded dogs, OK?"

Mary, as eager as ever to have Margaret pitch in notes, "Curtis, that Bernese Mountain Dog, Chloe, is here. She's been set up for a groom. Let's get her. Margaret, you can help me groom her. We'll start with a bath."

At dinner that night, Grayson seemed eager to know how the grooming went. "How'd it go today, kids?"

Margaret was the first to respond. "It went fine, Dad. I'm almost afraid to admit this but I sorta liked it."

Curtis immediately jumps in, "Told ya!"

"That doesn't mean I'm gonna continue to like it, Curtis."

"When you start making money, you'll like it more. Think of all the cartons of cigarettes you can buy."

"WHAT???????!!!!!!!!!!!! I do not smoke, you little shit ball!!!"

"Do too!"

Mother looks at them both with a blank stare, temporarily speechless. Then finally, "What???!!!"

"Mother, I do not smoke. I tried one once and Crude-Ass saw me trying it. It made me feel sick, and I don't like the taste. But I can think of plenty of other things I can do with the money. And Curtsie, if you're gonna start; let's bring up the subject of magazines under your mattress."

Curtis, having started this small conflagration decides to pull out of it before it gets worse. "I need to go. I have homework and I need to start calling some of these people that want me to show their dogs." He returns to his room, begins dialing his customers and diligently scribes several notes for future reference. Over the next several weeks, Curtis, Margaret, and Grayson spend many hours in the van driving from place to place, some over long distances. In the back of the van are crates with several dogs representing different breeds. At each show, Margaret diligently grooms while Curtis moves from one show ring to another. Grayson pitches in by delivering the dogs to their respective rings.

The Edwards family affair slowly becomes the talk of the dog show circuit. The young prodigy, Curtis, has mastered his craft. The hours and hours of training, development of style and technique, and the generation of a strong rapport with each of his canine friends have paid off. The ribbons and related prizes pour in as does the money. Curtis continues to experience some random acts of intimidation from other handlers, but he learns to retain his dignity by blowing off the insults, or merely responding in a judicious manner. Most of the rants from his fellow competitors are purely jealous acts focused on a young kid who showed them up with his self-acquired skills. Curtis feels that if all of the competitors made the same types of investment of time and effort, they too would experience the same results. Grayson had been instrumental in keeping Curtis focused on just being the best he could at his craft. But, he also reminded him that these acts are enhanced by the rapport he had developed with the animals.

"You see, Curtis, it simply appears that these dogs know you. They know you as more than their handler. They know you as their friend, someone who can purvey a sense of trust in them. They know that you are helping them succeed and it is evident on their faces and through their body language in the ring. I haven't seen anybody else that has shown me that. It all appears that it is no more than a business to most. Sure son, many of these handlers are attached to their dogs, but they are in it for the nickel, for the glory of having people recognize them as 'the handler to hire'. You do this for the love of the game, the love of the dogs, and to satisfy an inner passion. Hubcap gave you his heart and you did the same for him. He was a junkyard dog, Curtis, and now he's the best pet anyone could want. You won over your Mom and me. And, that devotion has trickled down to every other dog with which you enter those rings. Congratulations on that, and never lose sight of the fact that your passion must continue to be fueled by your actions in and outside of the ring. Does that all make sense to you?"

"It's a little heavy, Dad, but I see where you are coming from. I guess that I have become so absorbed in this that I don't think about anything else other than making these dogs and their owners very happy."

"And, you have son, believe me you have."

Chapter Six

Chicago, Illinois
(Twenty-four Years Later)

People with pets are milling around the waiting area of the Greater Chicago Animal Hospital, in the west side of Chicago. The Hospital has been in existence for over sixty years and wears its age quite well. The building is comprised of a burgundy brick façade with molded concrete trim. The grounds are perfectly manicured and a fenced-in dog run exists at the side of the building, convenient for a pet play area and a facility for "potty breaks". The interior is also spotless and it is evident that the clinic takes pride in its cleanliness and professional appearance. A large waiting area with ample seating appears as soon as one enters the front entrance. The reception area, "manned" by two uniformed employees sits to the rear of the waiting area. Curtis Edwards, now 39 years old, is the Hospital Administrator. A door to his office bears his name and his title. A veterinary assistant knocks on his door and enters.

"Hey Amy.. what's cookin'?"

"Curtis, Dr. Wilson just blasted my ass because we're running low on sutures andhe has six surgeries lined up for early next week. I tried to explain that I ordered them two weeks ago, but they just hadn't come in yet. Evidently it's my problem, not the vendor or UPS. Not sure what else we can do other than to borrow some from somewhere else."

"Hang on Amy, hang on. From whom did you order them?"

"Johnson Veterinary Supply"

"Just calm down, I've got that number right here."

Curtis dials the number and waits. Finally there is an answer from the other end of the line.

"Hello, this is Curtis Edwards from the Greater Chicago Animal Hospital. I'd like to speak to someone about an order." He is asked by a young fellow on the other end to hold. "OK, I'll hold." The other party returns to the phone. Having listened to what the fellow has to offer, Curtis responds. "They were sutures, we ordered two cases." The young man tells Curtis that they were shipped three days earlier. He proceeds to supply Curtis with a tracking number. "OK, let me read that back to you...KG7732983. Thank you and goodbye."

"Amy, hang on a minute more.. 'll call UPS."

"OK Curtis.. By the way, Dr. Wilson is a pain in my ass."

"He signs your check, Amy."

"Yeah, yeah, I know, I know. But it is accompanied by a mountain of unnecessary crap."

Curtis makes contact with UPS on the phone. It takes a while for anyone to pick up, but finally, "Hello, is this UPS? I need to track a shipment, please. The tracking number is KG7732983." It did not take long for the UPS representative to advise Curtis that the package would be delivered before ten o'clock AM the following day. Curtis relays this bit of good news to Amy.

"Curtis, you are the very best. If I weren't married, I'd give you a great big kiss!"

"Amy, even if you weren't married, I wouldn't be giving or receiving kisses to or from an employee."

"You're as straight as a loon's leg, Curtis....see you later."

At the end of the day, Curtis packs his briefcase and heads back to his apartment in downtown Chicago. As he enters his apartment, before he even has an opportunity to set the briefcase down, his cat quickly scrambles across the floor and nudges Curtis's leg for attention.

"Hey there, Nick. Miss your daddy today?"

Curtis's regular routine upon returning home is to change into some casual lounging clothes, head to the kitchen, and put out a bowl of food for "Nick, the Cat". Tonight is no different. For dinner he pulls some leftover mini-cartons of Chinese food out of the refrigerator. He assembles some morsels of the remaining delicacies on a plate, and sticks the plate in the microwave. He goes to his wine rack, pulls out a bottle of decent Cabernet, uncorks it, and pours himself a glass.

"Nicky, want to have a glass of wine with dad? You're the best date I've had in months." There is obviously no response from Nick, the Cat and one can only imagine that the only human word Nick knows is his name, Nick. Curtis turns the TV on and focuses on a Chicago Bulls basketball game. Armed with chopsticks, he eats his dinner, polishes off his wine, turns the TV off and picks up a Stephen King novel to read. Dozing off on the sofa, Curtis sets the book aside and heads for his bedroom. Nick, the Cat follows closely behind. Curtis curls up in bed and Nick curls up right at his side. It is not unusual for this happy ball of cat fur to end up under the covers on top of Curtis's feet. The following day, Curtis returns to the Animal Hospital with briefcase in hand. He is greeted by several of the staff and heads for his office. Almost immediately his phone begins to ring.

"This is Curtis Edwards, how may I help you?" Having listened to his caller, he responds that "Yes, we do orthopedic surgery here, but you need to be referred by your family veterinarian." The caller, obviously satisfied with his response bids adieu as does Curtis. "OK then, bye." Almost as soon as he hangs up, the phone rings again. This conversation centers around an order of toothbrushes and toothpaste of which Curtis's clinic only received half. After much confusion about payments, backorders, shipping, and whatever else could have created a problem with the order, Curtis hangs up, leans back in his flex-chair, and takes a long deep breath. Halfway through a relaxing exhale, there is a knock on his door.

"Come in.....Oh hi Marcy". Marcy is a front desk receptionist and general clinic administration clerk.

"Curtis, we have a 'situation' at the front desk. A lady is here with her Weimaraner and she learned that it needs ACL surgery. She can't afford it. I was honest with her Curtis. I told her that we can't make exceptions for payment. She doesn't want to put the dog down because it's only four years old, but she can't afford the two thousand dollars either. She wants to speak with a manager."

"Not sure what I can do, Marcy, but send her in. And, by the way, can you deflect my calls for a few minutes? My phone is ringing off the hook. I need a little break from that, oh, and thanks, Marcy."

The knock on the door is slight and quite tentative. Had Curtis been playing his radio or fidgeting with something, he would not have heard it.

"Please come in."

A woman enters Curtis' office. She has a handkerchief in hand and appears to be cleaning tears from under her eyes. She is about 5' 6" tall, lean figure, brunette hair, and quite attractive. Curtis looks up at her and raises his eyebrows. This situation was somewhat new to Curtis. He somehow knew what to expect, but he wasn't sure how he would handle it. Before the woman even had a chance to murmur one word, he agreed with himself to give the situation considerable thought before acting on it.

"Your dog has a torn ACL?"

"Lucy."

"OK, Lucy needs some surgery. And, may I ask what your name is?"

"It's Cyndi, Cyndi Gindy." Curtis's mouth immediately curled into a slight and partially disguised smile. "Who would name...? Oh, never mind, sorry. So how old is Lucy?"

"I know, I know...that's why I rarely tell people my last name. Not sure what Mom and Dad were thinking, well actually just Mom, Dad couldn't care less. He calls me 'sinner'."

Curtis, quite cognizant of the woman's distress tries to lighten the mood. "Is there a special reason why he calls you 'sinner'?"

"Ha! Not for the reasons you may think. He thinks it's a cutsie name for Cyndi. Lucy's four."

"How did Lucy hurt her knee?"

"Well, she was at the dog park with....by the way, what's your name?"

"Curtis, just call me Curtis.. that'd be fine."

"Hmmmm...Curtis...nice. Well, I was at the dog park with my neighbor Jimmy and his Golden Retriever, Deakie, and....."

"Deakie?????!!!Oh, sorry to interrupt."

"It's short for 'Deacon'. Jimmy and I were just sitting on the bench watching as Lucy and Deakie were running around, playing. All of a sudden, Lucy goes down, howling like a werewolf during a full moon, screaming like a banshee. I raced over there, and as she stood, I could tell that she was lame in the back and couldn't put any pressure on her right rear leg. Jimmy picked her up and carried her all the way back to the apartments and I walked Deakie home. We called my usual neighborhood vet and, upon his advice, brought her over there. They gave her some pain pills, but they said that they had to refer her to your hospital for evaluation. So, I was up with her all night, me and my poor baby, so here we are."

"I see. So the doctor told you that she needs surgery for a torn ACL?"

"Uh huh." Once again the tears begin to flow. "I am sorry; I just love her so much...she's my baby! I hope you can understand. I don't know what I would do if I had to put her to sleep. I couldn't stand the pain of losing her."

Curtis could immediately tell that the tears were authentic. Over his years, he had experienced tears for joy, tears for sadness, tears for fears, stress tears, tears for needs, baby tears, adult tears, alligator tears, and any other form of tears that have ever been shed. "And you don't have the money to pay for the procedure?"

Cyndi, working to hold back any further tears, "No, I don't."

Curtis immediately recognizes that he needs to regain his cheering up form, "Well I don't think we have any dishes that need to be washed."

Somewhere in between a sob and a chuckle at Curtis's remark, Cyndi claims, "I don't want to put her down. I can't."

"Ms. Gindy...."

"Please, it's Cyndi."

"Cyndi, here's what I would like to do. Let us keep Lucy overnight. You go home and try to relax your mind. We'll give her the very best of care and she won't have pain. I'll speak with the doctor to see if there is an alternative treatment. If not, maybe we can work something out, but I'll need the night to think about it. I'll call you first thing in the morning. Why don't you leave a number where you can be reached, or feel free to call me? Here's my card. Lucy will be just fine. That'll be my promise to you."

"Thank you, Curtis. Talk Tomorrow."

The next day arrives and Curtis is in his usual spot in his office contemplating life in general, Cyndi Gindy and her dog Lucy, and is peering out of the window. He plans to keep his promise to call Cyndi, but he hasn't yet determined what he would say. Curtis is somewhat hesitant to make special conditions as it could easily become habit forming. After sitting for a while, he notices that a pigeon has landed on his window sill. The pigeon bobs its head a few times and seems to turn its head to the right peering directly at Curtis. Curtis imagines the cooing as a request for food, but instead of obliging this curious bird, he picks up the phone and dials Cyndi Gindy's number.

"Hello, this is Cyndi."

"Hi Cyndi, this is Curtis Edwards from the Greater Chicago Animal Hospital."

"Hi Curtis, How's Lucy?"

"Lucy is fine, Cyndi. She wasn't in pain and she ate well which is a good sign. Cyndi, I've given a lot of thought to your dilemma. I even spoke with one of the surgeons this morning. The good news is that we can restore Lucy to good physical health, but the bad news is that the surgical procedure described to you is the only alternative."

"Oh my!"

"Well, I've given your personal situation some thought also. Let's see, the procedure is two thousand dollars and some change. We can't discount that but I can offer you a payment alternative. We generally would not consider this for most pet owners. So, if we can work something out, I would prefer if you did not discuss the terms with anyone. First, let me ask you, if you had to pay something on a weekly basis, how much could you afford to pay?"

"Uhmmmm, let's see...twenty-five dollars a week?"

"Well, that would take about a year and a half to pay. I was thinking more about fifty dollars a week. That way you would be paid up in ten months."

"I might be able to do that. I would have to cut back on some other things, but I'd do anything for Lucy; she's my life."

"OK then. Why don't you come in this afternoon and we can do some paperwork."

"Can I come in at five o'clock? I have an appointment that will be over at four-thirty and can make it over there by five."

"Sure, see you then."

At 5:00, Curtis looks up at the clock and almost simultaneously hears a knock on his door. Marcy is at the door leading Cyndi into Curtis' office. Cyndi is dressed in a chic, low cut, one piece dress with a flowing silk belt/sash. She is definitely a "fashion statement", a provocative one at that. Curtis wonders if this presentation is by design or if it is how she normally presents herself.

"Hi there, Cyndi. I've prepared some paperwork for you to sign. Lucy will have her surgery on Monday and she will convalesce here for two days. You can pick her up on Wednesday."

"I don't know how to thank you, Curtis. Please know how much I appreciate what you've done for Lucy and me."

"It is our pleasure."

Two days later, Cyndi enters the Animal Hospital to pick up Lucy. Marcy is attending the front desk and immediately recognizes Cyndi.

"Hi, I'm here to pick up Lucy Ginty."

"Of course, we'll have her out here in a few minutes. She'll be happy to see you. And, she has been a great patient."

"Sheepishly, Cyndi hands Marcy an envelope and asks, "Would you please give this envelope to Mr. Edwards?"

Marcy can wear a sly little smile with the best of them. She replies, "Of course, I'll see that 'Curtis' gets it."

"Thanks."

Within minutes, Lucy is being led on a leash to Cyndi, leg wrapped up, and a lampshade device on her head. As soon as Lucy spots Cyndi, her little tail starts to wag.

Marcy advises, "She'll have to wear the lampshade for a week. It's to keep her from pulling on the bandage. Also, be sure to have her move around slowly on a leash when you take her for her potty breaks, OK? Feed her half of what she usually eats but be sure she takes in a lot of water."

"No problem, I'll do that. Bye now."

Curtis is in his office working on some paperwork. Cyndi's card was delivered earlier, but Curtis opted to wait until the close of day to open it. It is a simple, elegantly embossed card with the letter "G" on it. There is a separate note inside. Curtis opens it and reads to himself.

Dear Curtis,

You can't imagine the gratitude I feel for what you have done for Lucy and me. I can see that you are the type of person who feels compassion for animals, of course, and other people as well. I am in the service industry, so I am well aware of the sacrifices we have to make daily to make others happy. I will always remember your kindness.

Fondly,
Cyndi G.

Curtis goes home that evening and drops his briefcase on the sofa. He reaches in and pulls out the card that Cyndi had left for him and places it on the counter. Nick, the Cat is there to greet him and meows for his dinner.

"You hungry there, Nickster?" As expected, the ritually generated meow responds to the question.

"OK, give me a minute, buddy and I'll get some food for you."

Curtis pulls out a can of cat food from the cabinet. Fish looks like a good option for the day. It is actually an option most of the days as Nick, the Cat usually inhales it. He's not as fond of chicken or any of the others for that matter. Curtis empties this culinary delight into Nick's bowl and then then pokes around the refrigerator for something for himself to eat. Almost jumping out to be consumed is a leftover package containing a giant Chinese wonton soup that Curtis had picked up on the way home two days earlier. Chinese food is a great option as his favorite spot is on his way home and the portions are large and inexpensive. Thus, Curtis's dinner is this tempting, always tasty bowl of wonton soup. It doesn't take very long at all for Curtis to devour the leftover soup. Now satiated, it is time to retire to the sofa where he is joined almost immediately by his faithful cat.

Having picked up Cyndi's card from the counter prior to collapsing on the sofa, he decides to give her a call. He had scribbled her number on an office pad and placed it in his briefcase, just in case. In case of what, he was not entirely sure. Curtis is well beyond the point where he needs courage to place such calls, so his hands were firm and sturdy throughout the process of pressing the number keys on the phone. Curtis hears the phone ringing and it is picked up by an answering machine.

"Hello, you've reached Cindy G. We are sorry that we are not available to accept your call right now, but in the event you are not a telemarketer or a sleazy caller who leaves obscene messages, please leave a message and your phone number, of course, and one of us will call you upon my return. Thank you."

Curtis thinks out loud, "WE???, One of us will call you back???"....beep...."Oh, Hi Cyndi, this is Curtis from the animal hospital. I am not trying to sell you anything, (well not yet anyway) nor am I going to breathe heavily through the phone. I just wanted to let you know that I received your thoughtful card and took the liberty to call just to say 'hi' and thank you too. If you would be so inclined to call me back, the number is 312.555.1199."Curtis places the phone back on its cradle and reaches for the TV remote. An episode of American Idol is on. He watches for a while. Nick, the Cat, also an American Idol aficionado is at his side. "Nickie, you can meow better than some of these people can sing."

Curtis picks up a Time Magazine and begins to leaf through the pages when his telephone rings.

Recognizing Cyndi's number on the caller ID, he answers almost immediately, "This is Curtis."

"Hi Curtis, it's Cyndi. I was so happy to hear your voice on the answering machine. I'm sorry but I was at Yoga class... Gotta keep my girlie figure ya know. I'm sorry that Lucy didn't pick up and tell you that I would soon be home."

"No, it's OK. I figured you were just busy with something. Nothing special."

In a very disappointed tone, "Nothing special? Awwww...."

"Well, so you appreciate an honest guy?"

"Course I do!"

"Well, when I met you, you seemed to be a sweet caring person and most importantly, you love animals. I don't do much socially, so I was thinking it might be nice if I could meet you for a dinner one night."

"Hmmmm...when were you thinking, Curtis?" Smiling a smile that Curtis cannot see, "Ya know I have a very busy schedule and I would have to see if I can squeeze you in."

"Dunno.. it seems like your schedule is the one we'll have to work around. Why not just tell me when you may be available."

"OK then, let me see. How about tomorrow night, or the night after that, or the night after that, or the night after that?" Cyndi is hard pressed to withhold some gentle laughter that Curtis quickly picks up on.

"Yah, Tomorrow night will work, Cyndi". Would you be able to meet me, say around seven o'clock at Wilson's Tavern on Rush Street downtown? Heard of it?"

"Heard of it? Ha! I am on their beer taster's email list. They have periodical features of beers from around the world. Sure, I'll be there! I'll leave Lucy at home. Anyway, she doesn't like parading around in public with the lampshade. She is quite vain, ya know! And she quit drinking beer a while back. See you tomorrow, Curtis. And don't bring your beer goggles. Somehow I don't think you'll need them."

"I think I already knew that. See you then, Bye."

The following evening, Curtis walks into Wilson's Tavern with clean cut jeans and a nice micro- fiber shirt. He looks around and spots Cyndi, already sipping on a beer at a table half way down the right side of the wall. Cyndi is also dressed in jeans with a beige pullover sweater, discreetly covering a shapely contour.

"Hey Cyndi, got a jump start on me?"

"Hi Curtis! I can never gauge how long it would take to get down here, and I wanted to be punctual, so here I am. Only been here seven or eight minutes. Sit down. Get comfortable."

"Thanks. Whatchya drinking?"

"It's a Costa Rican beer. It's called Imperial. Quite tasty. Want a sip? It's OK, you can drink from my glass, and the herpes is all cleared up now."

"Nice. Well thanks; I'll just get one also."

A smartly clad waitress finds her way over to Curtis and Cyndi's table. "May I get you something to drink, sir?"

"Yah, thanks. I'll have one of those Imperials also."

"Good choice. It'll be right up. Another for you ma'am?"

"No, I'm good. I'll nurse this a while longer. But, why not bring us one of those appetizer samplers? OK? Thanks."

With a wide grin, Cyndi remarks, "Glad you called, Curtis."

"Me too."

"Where do we start, Curtis?"

"Want to tell me about growing up in Gindyville?"

"Funny, Curtis. Well, I grew up in the area, Rockford actually. I went to high school there and tried college for a few years. It didn't agree with me. It wasn't like I couldn't get through it; I just don't think my mind set was to sit behind books for another few years. One day, I saw an advertisement in the Chicago Gazette for flight attendants. So, I called the number, they called me back and invited me back for an interview. The rest is history, so I've now been flying with North American Airlines for the past 16 years."

"Do you like it?"

"It's OK. Not all it's 'cracked up to be'. I could tell you a lot of stories. I'll wait until we get to know one another better before I burden you with that."

"Anyone ever join the 'mile high' club while you were working?"

"That's a strange question for our first encounter, but Ha! Oh yeah! Once. And the circumstances were bizarre. They didn't even know each other when the flight took off. We flight attendants had a fun one with that. I'll tell you more about that some other time. What about you, Curtis?"

"Whoa, me? No, I've never joined the mile high club."

"I didn't mean that, silly! Tell me something about you."

"Well, I've been with the Animal Hospital for ten years. I grew up in Gary, Indiana, went to high school there. My parents still live there. I have an older sister, Margaret. She's working in New York City for an advertising firm. I went to college at U. of Illinois in Champagne. I always loved pets, especially dogs, so I decided that my life would revolve around them. I wanted to be a vet, but I didn't have the grades."

"Why not? You seem quite bright. Otherwise you're a good actor."

"Well, this may seem unusual to you Cyndi, but I've had a job since I was 14 years old. When I'm not working at the animal hospital, I'm a dog handler at various dog shows."

"Interesting."

"Yah, it's interesting alright, but it takes up all of my time. I am not as heavily into it as I was before, but I am still doing it almost every weekend. That's why I couldn't get the grades to go to veterinary school. I was just too busy with the dog handling. The money was very good, so I didn't want to give it up. I was lucky to have gotten through undergraduate school. I did major in Animal Science though, so it made it easier for me. The dog handling bit has also had an impact on my social life. I'm just not around enough to get involved with much else. I'm not sure I should have shared that with you."

"Well, that's sad, Curtis."

"Well, I have dated off and on over the years, and I have had a few girlfriends, but those relationships never lasted. I wasn't able to give them enough time."

Cyndi hesitates for a brief while before responding. She cocks her head slightly to the left and with a non-discernable look on her face, asks, "Should I just 'throw in the towel' now?"

Curtis gets a brief chuckle from that question. "What about you? Any love interests, Cyndi?"

"I was engaged up until two years ago. He is a pilot. I met him while he was 'dead heading' on a flight. Great guy. As time went on, I learned that he had other love interests and a former wife that I never knew about. He also enjoyed a cocktail now and then, oftentimes to a greater extent than was necessary. Admittedly, he never violated the 'eight hour from cocktail to cockpit rule', but when he was off and drank, he would often become belligerent. I ended it a few years ago. I gave him back his ring, but he wouldn't accept it. So, it sits in a jewelry box at home. I have dated a few guys over the past few years but it's the same old story...gotta kiss a lot of frogs before you find a prince". Pausing again for a few seconds, she asks "Are you my prince, Curtis?"

"Dunno. I guess it's too early to decide that."

"Well, that's true. I suppose time will tell."

"When do you fly again?"

"Not until next weekend. I bid for International this month, so I only really fly three trips, but they are grueling. The good news is that I am only gone four days at a time. Jimmy, my neighbor, watches after Lucy while I am away."

"Any love interest with Jimmy?"

That question strikes a funny chord with Cyndi as she laughs out loud. "No, no. He's younger than me. And I just don't think he could ever have those types of feelings for me. You'll meet him, you'll see. Great guy!!! He gives a great haircut too! Curtis, want to take a walk? We can go over to North Michigan Avenue and walk down the beach. People take their dogs there to play. It's beautiful in the evening."

"Sure, let's go."

Curtis and Cyndi walk north on Michigan Avenue. Sometimes instincts deliver messages that in some cases should be ignored, and in other cases should be received with gratitude. Curtis receives a message that he shouldn't waste any time with Cyndi. As they walk up the Avenue, Curtis reaches out to hold her hand. And, Cyndi willingly grasps Curtis' hand.

As if nothing had changed Curtis asks, "Hungry?"

"No, you?"

"No, I'm gastronomically satiated. The appetizers did the trick."

"Trying to impress me with your vocabulary?"

"Well Cyndi, it just sounded better than... 'FULL'."

"Do you have a dog at home?"

"No. I had one once. His name was 'Hubcap'. Found him in a junkyard. Long story. I just don't have the time. It would be unfair to a dog to have one now. I'm hardly ever home. I do have a cat though. His name is Nick, the Cat."

"Cute."

"You can meet him sometime if you would like."

"Would Love to!"

Arriving at the shore line for Lake Michigan, they find a bench to sit on and look out at the silhouettes of people walking, some with dogs frolicking about near them.

"Ya know, Curtis, I come here by myself a lot. I like to sit and just look out at the lake. This will sound corny, but there is something peaceful about this lake. It is windy, often frigid, vast, but somehow alluring. I look out and think about the things I have done, should have done, shouldn't have done, and things I want to do. This is as good a place as any to think about those things." Curtis is looking directly into her eyes as she speaks. Cyndi pauses for about a minute before resuming, neither of them saying a word. "I think about all of the people I see out here and wonder about each of their stories. I'll bet their lives run the entire gamut. And, I see myself in between all of that. Not rich, not poor. Not unhappy, but not terribly thrilled. Not unintelligent, but not a 'Jeopardy! Contestant' either. The Lake doesn't talk back to me when I ponder out loud, but it has its own story to tell me. So, I sit and pretend to listen to what it tells me. Rhetorically speaking, does that make sense? It tells me about the people who have walked its shores over the ages, the fishermen, the stranded, the lost, the storms, the sunrises and sunsets, and much more. . . . Am I boring you, Curtis?"

"No, not at all. I enjoy listening. Maybe I should spend more time managing and interpreting my thoughts."

"I do it all of the time. They had a side class at Yoga, so I learned Meditation. You should try it."

"Maybe I will. I'll need to get up early, Cyndi. Maybe I should walk you back to your car."

"Sounds good."

Curtis never lets go of Cyndi's hand on the stroll back to her car. A brief hug with each sharing a small kiss on the cheek concludes the evening.

"Was great, Cyndi."

"Yah, was great. Nite, Curtis."

"Nite, Cyndi."

The following day is routine like the others for Curtis, but he felt an inner joy that he had missed for the longest time. In his office, leaning back in a chair, his hands behind is head, staring at the ceiling, he reviews the previous few days when he hears the phone ring.

"This is Curtis Edwards."

"This is Cyndi G."

"Hey Cyndi."

"I just wanted to thank you for meeting me last night. I had a great time, and I enjoyed learning a little about you."

"The feeling is mutual."

"Curtis, with some fear of sounding forward, I was wondering what you are doing tonight."

"Uhmm, no plans, what did you have in mind?"

"I have an idea and I want you to join me."

"Sure...I'm game."

"Meet me at 1229 Centre Street at seven o'clock sharp. You can find it easily. Bring a pair of shorts, some tennis shoes, a T-shirt, and a towel."

"Yikes, I'm not the best with surprises, but okay, but I'll be there at seven sharp."

"See you there."

Curtis was well aware of what Yoga was but had never tried it. In his mind, it consisted of contorting one's body into a group of positions, most of which Curtis believed his body would respond with a huge lack of cooperation. Nonetheless, when love is in the air, it tends to transcend into other places including the side by side mats that he and Cyndi now occupied. The earliest of exercises, supposedly the warm-up variety and the easiest of all seemed to be indisputably intense to Curtis. He does his best to hide the grimaces that the pain has generated. After yoga, Curtis and Cyndi walk to a local pub to have a post-Yoga beer. Now inside the pub, Curtis remarks that he isn't quite sure if Cyndi is a sadist or if he is a masochist.

"I thought I would try to interest you in some of the things I enjoy doing."

"Oh really!!!?? Okeydokey then, well, when do you want to go to a dog show?"

"Any time, Curtis, just give me some advanced notice."

"I'm handling a few dogs in a show this weekend up in the Milwaukee area. Care to join me?"

"I can't Curtis, I'm flying. But I promise I'll go after I get back."

"Oh right, I believe you told me that already. But, after you return sounds good to me. I think you would have enjoyed it. Some beautiful breeds will be there and there are some high quality dogs in the show, including a few that I'll be handling, I might add."

"Now I'm really sorry I'll be gone."

"Hey, I'm completely worn out. But, I do have enough energy for just one game of darts. Wanna play?"

"Don't know how...."

"It's easy, I'll show you."

Curtis retrieves a few sets of darts from the bartender and heads back over to the dart board. He hands Cyndi three of one color and keeps three for himself.

"There are a few different games you can play, Cyndi, but for the purposes of this lesson, we'll just try to concentrate on getting the darts near the bull's-eye, OK?"

"Okay, but not to sound too stupid, the bull's-eye is the red circle right smack in the middle, right?"

"Yes, but somehow I believe you already knew that." Cyndi merely looks at Curtis with a sheepish grin and suggests they get started. "OK Cyndi, start by standing behind this line on the floor. Then, holding the dart between your thumb and your forefinger, eye the bull's-eye and pull the dart back behind your ear like this. Then, let it fly towards the target, whoosh."

Curtis's dart sails across the play area and lands near the perimeter of the target. The next two aren't much better, but at least one is somewhere near the center.

"Well, that wasn't great, but I think you get the idea, right?"

"Right, I think I get it. My turn?"

"Yup, let 'em fly."

Cyndi rears back, holds the dart in the recommended position, then lets it fly. The first dart lands right next to the bull's-eye.

"Wow, what about that Curtis? I was lucky with that one, right?"

"That was great for a first-timer. You still have two more though. Just do everything the same way as you did the first time."

Cyndi throws the second dart and it lands just on the other side of the bull's-eye, exactly perpendicular with the first dart. Curtis stands speechless with a look of surprise and wonder in his face. Cyndi launches the third dart and it lands directly inside the middle of the bull's-eye.

"Okay this might have to call for a spanking, Cyndi!! What other tricks do you have up your sleeve??"

"Well, maybe someday you'll know. Ready to go?"

"Yah, ready….brat face."

Curtis and Cyndi bid adieu for the evening. Returning to his apartment, the rush of excitement over recent social events leaves him distracted and not tired. It is time for a shower after which he climbs onto his sofa. Nick, the Cat jumps up on the sofa with him and snuggles at his side.

"What do you want to watch there, Nick? Okie dokie then, lets' watch a movie...You pick it." Nick meows......"No, no, we're not watching 'The Lion King' again."

Chapter Seven

Staten Island, New York

Caroline Alonzo, aged 14, and her father, Tommy Alonzo, are driving home from school in his black Lincoln sedan.

"Dad, why did you pick me up from school today? Where's Mom?"

Tommy is in his early 40's, round in places that suggest he enjoys a good meal as often as possible, and carries a New York style Italian accent, not unlike that which one might hear while watching a mob-type film. "I dunno, she had some kinda nail appointment or somethin' like that. I happened to be home working on somethin'.You in a hurry, Caroline? I gotta pick up some stuff at the Hardware Depot. It'll only take a 'coupela' minutes."

"I don't care, Dad…Can I go in there with you?"

"Yeah, sure."

They leave the car and both notice a pickup truck in the parking lot, a few parking spots away from where they are parked. From the short distance, Caroline can see that there is a small temporary metal dog enclosure with some puppies running around inside it.

"Look Dad, the guy's got puppies."

"Yeah, good, great, let's go shopping."

"No, c'mon Dad, I want to see the puppies."

"Okay, two minutes, I gotta get outta here. I've got things I need to do."

The two walk over to the older model black pickup. Caroline seems to be in more of a hurry to get over there than Tommy and arrives at the pickup first. A man in his thirties wearing a baseball cap, sweatshirt, and jeans greets them. There is one other person, a woman, looking at the puppies.

Tommy was the first to inquire. In an imposing tone, "Whaddiya got here?"

The baseball capped fellow responds with "These are registered Black Lab puppies."

"Yeah, registered with what? Registered to vote?" Tommy enjoys his retort so much as to laugh out loud.

Facetiously, the fellow pretends a returning chuckle, "A haha! No, the NKA."

"The NKA! What the freak is that!!??"

The fellow is already exasperated with having to answer the questions, but advises Tommy that it is The National Kennel Association.

"Yeah, OK, good. We gotta go, Caroline."

"I want one, Dad."

"They probably got them worms or somethin'."

Offended, baseball cap guy jumps in, "They've already been wormed by a vet, mister."

"Yeah? Well whoopdedoo. Let me ask you something there pal. You married?"

"I am. Why would you ask me that? And, why do you care?"

"How'd your wife like it if she sent you out on a errand with your little girl and came home with a freakin' puppy?"

"My wife would most likely not mind mister; she loves dogs."

"Yeah, ya know what? Mine would freakin' kill us."

"Well you obviously have interest, at least the little girl does, and otherwise you wouldn't have come over here."

"Hey, gumbatz, she just wanted to see the things. She didn't say nothin' about buying one. Let's go, Caroline. I gotta get some stuff and we gotta get home before your mother gets back from the pamperin' place."

"That's a nail salon, Dad."

"Yeah, OK, whatever."

Not forgetting their original mission, Caroline and Tommy spend some time in the Hardware Depot and leave with an assortment of small garden tools and other miscellaneous supplies. The same night, the three are sitting around the dinner table, eating and engaging in a rather quiet conversation of the day's events. Caroline's mother, Corinne, a somewhat pragmatic woman in her early 40's, opens the conversation.

"Thanks for picking up Caroline from school, Tommy." She raises both hands in the air and asks, "Like my nails?"

Without even offering the courtesy of turning his head in his wife's direction, in a highly sardonic manner, Tommy responds "Yeah, gorgeous."

Corinne, offended, suggests "I don't even know why I bother telling you anything. You couldn't give a crap anyway."

"Hey, hey watch it! I said gorgeous, didn't I?"

"You didn't mean it and you weren't even looking at me."

"Geez honey…"

"Watch it Tommy! Don't be using the name of the Lord in vain."

"I didn't say shit! What is this? Prosecute Tommy day?"

"It's persecute, Tommy, persecute for crying out loud. And, no, you are not being persecuted. I would just appreciate a little respect once in a while. How about we just finish eating in peace and get on with it?"

Caroline feels the need to jump in and put an end to this minor, highly unnecessary fray. "Mom, there was a man with puppies at the Hardware Depot today."

Corinne looks in Caroline's direction, and offers, "Yeah, so?"

Tommy of course feels compelled to jump in. "See, Caroline??!!"

"See what, Dad?"

"See, your Mom doesn't give a crap either."

"I didn't say I didn't give a crap, Tommy. What were you going to tell me, honey?"

"I think I am old enough and responsible enough now. I want a puppy."

"I'm not sure we're all ready for that, honey. But, we can think about it. I know you like dogs."

"Mom, every time I bring it up, Dad makes some stupid joke about it. I am dead serious."

It becomes Tommy's time to insert his two cents worth. "Yeah, wanna know why sweet pea? Cause as soon as you get a little older, and you start discovering boys, and doin' whatch you teenagers do, guess who's gonna be taking care of your little puppy."

"That's not fair, Daddy, at least let me try it. If it isn't working out, we can find it a home. But, I know it'll work out, I really know that, Daddy. I am doing well in school. I get good grades all of the time. I don't run around the streets like a lot of other kids."

"Yeah? Then who's gonna take the dog out for a walk at night. You ain't gonna go out there at night alone with a dog. There's a lot of creepos out there these days."

"We have a yard, Dad."

"Oh, great, the dog is gonna crap all over my yard now?"

"I'm leaving. I'm not hungry any more, Mom. I'll be in my room." Caroline gets up from the dinner table, walks out of the room and heads for her bedroom. In her mind, she wasn't playing the martyr; she had always wanted a puppy and her disappointment in her father's response has crushed her dream.

Corinne is torn but knows that it has been something Caroline had been thinking about for quite some time. "Tommy, maybe we should consider a pet for Caroline. She deserves it. She's a great kid, she doesn't get in any trouble, she does well in school, and she is very helpful around the house. She never asks for anything. I vote that at least we give it a try."

"Ya know what??!! The two of youse work it out. Just don't make me do all the hard stuff."

"I'm going to help her, Tommy. I won't let her make a bad decision about this."

The following day Corinne is driving Caroline to school. She knew quite well that Caroline was still a bit distraught over her Dad's position.

"Honey, your father and I discussed this puppy thing after you left dinner last night."

"And??"

"We think that we'll let you give it a try, PROVIDING, of course that you are responsible about it, and that it doesn't mean a lot of work for all of us. That's your Dad's biggest concern. He doesn't want to become the custodian of a dog right now, or ever for that matter."

"A dog should be a family pet, Mom, not just mine."

"I can tell you right now, honey, that your father isn't going to have much to do with it."

"How can anyone not love a puppy??!!"

"Honey, here we are at school. Have a great day. And oh, to answer your question, everybody loves a puppy. But they grow up to be dogs, just like kittens grow up to be cats. They are not cute and cuddly forever."

"I do not agree, Mom, but I know it will work out great, actually better than great!"

Two days pass and during dinner Caroline brings up the issue of a puppy again. "I bought a book today at the book store. It's about puppies. I'll study it so that I won't make any mistakes."

Tommy, in a much more conciliatory tone, asks, "What kind you thinking about getting, honey?"

"I'm not sure yet, Dad. There's so much to learn. Every breed has its own personality. I need to find one that fits into our lifestyle and will be fun. I want one that will be my companion, one that will always be happy to see me when I get home every day. There's one more book I want to get, but I don't have the money right now. It is from the National Kennel Association and it has pictures of every breed and tells you everything about every dog. I may try to borrow it from the library. They'll probably have it."

"Corinne, take Caroline to the library tomorrow. If they don't have the book, go to the book store. I'll pay for it."

"Thanks, Dad. I love you."

"Me too, baby. I gotta hurry up. The guys are coming over for our Thursday night card game."

Corinne, highly cognizant of this recurring event is not terribly pleased to hear this news, but accepts it. "Can you guys for once not leave a big stinkin' mess down there, because I am the one that has to clean it up? And, I might add that the basement stinks of cigars all the time."

"Where else we supposed to go?"

"One of the other guys houses, Tommy. They live somewhere. You can stink up some other place. Give our place a break for a change."

"They like it here. More privacy and better food."

"Yeah, well guess what! The food is coming to a screeching halt! Tell them to bring some take-out or something. I'm tired of cooking for those guys."

"They appreciate your cookin', honey."

"I didn't say they didn't appreciate it. I said I was tired of it. Tommy, you're a royal pain in my ass...ya know that?"

"OK, OK, fuggetaboutit! I'll call Louie to pick up some Chink food or something."

"Chink food? Really??!! Nice Tommy! Yeah, you do that."

Four dark haired men, none of which would qualify as a "Weight-Watcher" spokesperson, are sitting around eating Chinese food out of the cartons. Louie, Marco, Tony, and Tommy, all in their 40's, are stuffing these Asian delights in their faces and making typical grunt-like consumption sounds. Three of them are eating with forks, Louie is eating with chopsticks.

"Hey Louie, what are you, a fuggin' showoff or something, eating with the fuggin pencils?" Tommy's comment drew a chuckle from the others.

"Hey, when in Rome, do what the fuggin Romans do."

"Romans? What fuggin Romans? We're in fuggin Staten Island you shit for brains."

Marco jumps in, "Hey, shuddup already. Let's finish eatin' so I can take youse money."

Tommy of course questions Marco's use of the English language. "Youse money?"

Marco retorts with, "Hey. Mr. Median Webster or whatever that dictionary guy's name is. You speak the best English? Gimme a fuggin break here. In fact, I hear you saying 'youse' all of the time, so calm down your yapper."

Apparent ringleader Tommy, probably because it is his house in which they sit, calls out to Louie. "Hey, Louie, before we start. What's goin' on with the vending machine distribution on Second Avenue?"

"It's goin' OK. It's getting tougher and tougher boss. A lot of resistance. A lot of these people just don't get it. A lot of friggin foreigners over there, too."

Tommy grimaces at this response. "So, fuggin educate 'em."

"Ain't that easy boss. Like for example, four days ago I send two of my boys over to this new Japanese restaurant on Second. It's downstairs below street level. Sose they go down there and tell the owner, some skinny Jap lady, about 45 years old, that they're delivering a juke box to her. Well, the lady says, 'I no order juke box'. Sose, the boys say, 'Look lady, you don't understand. This is free; we bring it down here, we plug it in, and every week, we come and pick up the cashola. We split it 50- 50, so lady, you're making money and you don't have to do shit.' So, then she says,'No, you no understand. I have karaoke here. No need jukebox.' Sose anyway the boys go to the truck, unload the fuggin jukebox, and start taking it down the stairs. She starts fuggin screaming like someone just ripped off her Geisha fuggin outfit. 'I told you no jukebox!! I calling police now!! 'Sose the boys splain to her that calling the police would be a very bad idea, and they leave. Two days later, they come back and the fuggin jukebox is unplugged. Sose one of my boys says to her, 'Look you friggin idiot, you don't fuggin get it, do you??!!. You get half the money'. She says, 'I no want your money, I want that thing out!' Sose, they leave. Late that night, there's an accident at the restaurant in the middle of the night. The fuggin glass door gets busted up, and some rocks with some impolite friggin notes get tossed through the window downstairs. I'm sure she called the cops but they ain't gonna do nothin', never do. See what we have to deal with now?"

Marco, listening attentively mentions, "I have the same shit with some video games, the kind we put on the bars. One guy tells me that if I put the fuggin machine at the bar, that keeps one person from drinkin' because it takes up the space where a seat is and he can't make no money off them. I told him, hey moron, they fuggin drink when they play those games. You end up with even more money cause you get half the take."

Louis mentions that "You gotta be a fuggin sales expert anymore."

Tommy, taking this all in asks, "How many new machines we got on Second Avenue now?"

Tony gets to speak for the first time. "Hey, I don't know nothing about Second Avenue but we have about thirty new machines in Chinatown."

Tommy, in his most pedantic manner says, "That's cause the Chinks don't fuck with us. We help them, they help us. We protect them when they sell them fake fuggin watches and handbags, and shit. They let us stick our machines in their fine establishments."

Marco, eager to take his buddies money jumps in, "OK, let's cut the bullshit and play some cards."

Chapter Eight

Corinne and Caroline are at the Staten Island Library looking for the book published by the National Kennel Association. Corinne approaches the Librarian.

"Ma'am, do you have a reference book published by the National Kennel Association about different breeds of dogs?"

Pointing in the direction of a group of shelves, the librarian tells Corinne that "If we do, it will be in the last section of books, closest to the aisle in the third row over there."

Corinne and Caroline peruse the books until they finally come across what they are seeking.

"Mom, this book is about 25 years old. Look how tattered it is. I am not sure this information is up to date."

"Yah, looks kinda scruffy, honey. Let's go to the bookstore. There's a Smart's Books down the street."

Smart's Books is a major chain and has a huge selection of books in their pet section. Corinne and Caroline examine many of the books. It didn't take long to find exactly what they seek.

"Wow, forty bucks, Caroline, but if it is what you want, let's go for it. Your father said that he would pay for it."

The ride home could not go quickly enough for Caroline. Once they arrive at home, Caroline heads straight to her room where she sits on the bed going through every picture, every description. Eventually, the clock is passing through the hours of the night and she is getting practically no sleep trying to find her dream dog. Day breaks, and with little sleep to speak of, Caroline makes her way down to the breakfast table. Corinne and Tommy are already there eating.

"Mom, Dad, I think I found the dog I was looking for."

Tommy was the first to demonstrate interest. "Yeah, what??!!"

"It's called a Golden Retriever. They look beautiful, and listen to the description: Shrewd, great endurance, reliable, intelligent, easygoing, great family pet, good with children, excellent watchdog, loyal, and even-tempered. This is the dog I want."

Tommy, eager to get this mission behind the family, suggests, "So, go to the pet shop and pick one up."

"OK, wow, let's go tomorrow, OK?"

The local Staten Island pet shop, "Paws and Claws", is known for their high standards and houses every type of household creature that is not considered human. Corinne and Caroline enter through the front door and quickly bypass the hamsters, fish, snakes, and rabbits. The dogs are in the back in clean cages with plenty of toys and other distractions to keep them busy. As they approach the dogs, a few heads peer out from their enclosures, slumber behind them, and tails begin to wave. It appears to be a happy bunch. A pet store associate, eager to assist, walks over to where they are standing in front of the dog pens.

"Looking for anything in particular?"

Caroline knows exactly what she is looking for. "Yes, I want a Golden Retriever."

"I'm sorry miss but we don't have any Goldens right now. We had the last one go out yesterday. But, we should be getting some in next month. The puppies usually come in once a month. I am able to put a hold on one for you if you would like."

"But I want one now. Where can I find one?"

"Well, you can call some other pet stores, but if you do, be certain that it is a reputable shop. Or, call the National Kennel Association. They can tell you if there are any local breeders around."

"OK, thanks, bye."

Back at home, Caroline finds the phone number of the National Kennel Association and dials the number. The phone is picked up after the third ring.

An operator with a pleasant voice answers. "Good afternoon and thank you for calling the NKA. May I help you?"

"Yes, my name is Caroline Alonzo and I heard that someone in your office can tell me how to find a breeder of Golden Retrievers."

"Well, thank you for thinking of us, but we're not in the business of recommending breeders. I can put you through to one of our show coordinators and maybe they can help you. Please hold for just a moment."

Another voice comes on the phone. "This is Susan, how may I help you?"

"I am trying to find out if there is a breeder of Golden Retrievers near where I am."

"Okay, sure, I can check. Where are you located?"

"I live in Staten Island, New York."

"Okay, very well then, let me think. Uhmm, you know, there are several good breeders in the area, for all different kinds of breeds. I do have an idea for you. Do you know where Morristown, New Jersey is?"

"No, but I am sure that my Mom or Dad knows."

"Well, there is a show there this weekend at the Morristown Memorial Park. If you can get out there, buy a catalogue when you enter. Go to the ring for the breed you want to see. Did you say Golden Retriever?"

"Yes."

"Ok then. Look at the dogs in the ring and see which one looks the best to you. Don't worry about which one wins or loses. Just get a feel for what you want to see in your dog, and make a choice that way. The handler will be wearing a number on his or her sleeve. Get the number and look in the catalogue for the corresponding number next to the name of the dog. After the description of the dog, the name of the owner will follow. You can find out how to contact the owner by looking up their name and address in the back of the catalogue. Or, easier yet, just speak with the dog's handler. They are usually cordial unless they are in a hurry to show another dog."

"Thank you so much!!"

"It was my pleasure."

The drive to New Jersey was less tedious than Corinne and Caroline expected. Tommy had stayed behind in order that he could catch up with some "business issues". Caroline is somewhat adept at reading maps. She is following every turn with as much accuracy as can be expected.

"Mom, I think you have to turn left at the next light."

"Got it, honey."

"Hey Mom, look. That's it!! See all of the tents and vans?"

The show grounds are vast. There are several tents used for registration, judge's quarters, refreshments, first aid, and more. Surrounding the tents are several show rings, each with a table and a few chairs alongside the tables. Corinne and Caroline pay an entrance fee at the gate and buy a catalogue. Caroline immediately thumbs through the catalogue in search of the venue for Golden Retrievers. They are looking at the pages for Golden Retrievers.

"Mom, Golden Retrievers come on at one o'clock in Ring Five."

"We'll have time for lunch then, honey. Look, over there, it's a food stand. You hungry?"

"Yup." Laughing out loud, "Wonder if they have hot dogs??!!"

"You're almost as funny as your father, honey."

The snack bar was a welcome sight to both. They had a wait on their hands and they were both quite hungry. After sharing a tuna salad sandwich and a sack of potato chips, they take a walk through a line of vendors that are adjacent to the eating area. Caroline eyeballs a book at one of the vendors that is specifically about Golden Retrievers. Corinne opens her handbag and pays for it. They then walk over to Ring Five where Golden Retriever judging is about to begin. The judge is a matronly woman in her fifties and is preparing to begin looking at the puppy class. Caroline stares intently as the young puppies enter the ring. She waits patiently for the older dogs to begin to assemble. After the puppy class is over the older males enter the ring. According to the catalogue, these are the "Open Dogs", ones that have not yet finished their championship.

"Oh Mom, they're gorgeous!!!!"

"Wow, you're right. I never knew. I have seen these types of dogs out and about but never ones that look like some of these. Are you sure this is the breed you want, honey?"

"I knew it just as soon as I saw them. I have never been more certain about anything. There's nothing out here that is prettier."

"Honey, let's wait for the champions to come out; then we'll see if there's one you like better than the rest. I hope they'll talk to us."

Corinne and Caroline patiently watch as the classes of Golden Retrievers are judged. It finally comes time for the champions to enter the ring. One by one they enter for a total of ten. Each is as beautiful as the others.

"Mom, I don't know who the judge will select, but I am sure I have the winner."

"Me too sweetie, me too!!"

"Which one, Mom?"

"Third one from the left."

Caroline reaches up to "high five" Corinne. The dogs go through their routine with the judge, and sure enough, the dog they both picked won. As the handler of the winning dog leaves the ring, Corinne and Caroline approach her. At the same time, others join the handler to congratulate her.

Corinne edges her way up to the handler, "Congratulations!"

Slightly winded, the handler replies, "Thanks!"

Corinne is as eager as Caroline to learn more about the dog she handled. "I am sorry, I do not know you name, I am Corinne, and this is my daughter Caroline beside me here. May we talk to you about your dog?"

"Sure, I would be happy to. My name is Elizabeth by the way. Let me put him up first. I'll be back over here in ten minutes."

Corinne and Caroline wait patiently for Elizabeth's return. Ten minutes later, Elizabeth is back at ringside chatting with some people. When the timing seems right, Corinne and Caroline approach her.

"Is now a good time, Elizabeth, to talk to you about your dog?"

"Oh, yes, I'm sorry. I guess I got caught up in the moment."

Caroline is most eager to get some answers and jumps right in. "I want my first puppy and I know I want a Golden Retriever. Your dog was the prettiest one we saw."

"Well, you've picked a great breed. That dog is one of the country's top Goldens, now. His name is Charlie. But actually, his NKA name is Goldmark's Carlton of Rosemeade."

Corinne responds, "Wow, that's a mouthful. Is he yours?"

"Actually, no. I just show him. He's owned by Susan Claiborne out in a town called Watchung, also in New Jersey, not far from here. She was here a while ago...that's who I was talking to when I left the ring with him. I'd spend more time with you, but I have to get into the Westie ring. Susan's name and address are in the catalogue. She always welcomes a call. She's proud of her boy here. See ya."

Both Corinne and Caroline say goodbye simultaneously.

"Ready to go home, Caroline?"

"Ready when you are, Mom."

Later in the evening, Corinne takes the initiative of calling Susan Claiborne. Caroline is sitting right by her side and would not miss the opportunity to listen in on the conversation. The phone on the other end rings and a middle-aged sounding woman's voice answers.

"May I speak to Susan Claiborne please?"

"I am Susan speaking."

"Hi Ms. Claiborne, my name is Corinne Alonzo and I am calling you from Staten Island, New York."

"Call me Susan."

"Oh, OK, Susan. My daughter and I were at the show today and saw Charlie win. It was out first dog show. He is gorgeous."

"Why, thank you. I am very proud of my boy. He is a multi 'Best in Show' winner and has a great disposition."

"My daughter wants a puppy and she knows that she wants it to be a Golden Retriever."

"Good choice, Corinne."

"Well, I don't want to take a lot of your time, but do you know where we can find a puppy that will ultimately someday look like Charlie?"

"Well, there's no guarantee that any dog will look like Charlie. He's one of a kind. But, I can tell you that he was bred to a bitch in Mahwah, New Jersey. There were eight puppies but I don't know if they are all spoken for. I can give you the telephone number of the owner of the bitch and she can tell you if she has any available. They should be good puppies. Charlie is OFA Certified, the bitch is also, and she is clear of brucellosis."

Corinne gently covers the speaker part of the phone and whispers over to Caroline. "She's speaking Greek to me but I think I have a lead."

Susan continues, "Her name is Claudia Strong and her number is….hmmmm…let me see….OK, yes, here it is…201.555.3371."

"Thanks, Susan, I'll call her now."

"Good luck to both of you. Bye now."

Corinne and Caroline are once again in the car driving north into New Jersey. They arrive at the house of Claudia Strong. They are greeted by Claudia at her front door and taken to the garage in the back where there is a temporary kennel with eight puppies running around looking for something with which to play.

Caroline is obviously quite excited. "May I go in there with them?"

"Sure, but prepare yourself. They enjoy the company."

Caroline enters the kennel and all eight puppies run up to her. One larger male seems to want to paw Caroline. Caroline picks him up and holds him tight. Caroline's smile couldn't grow any wider than it already was. She bears a bona fide ear to ear grin. She asks, "Are they all sold?"

"Six of them are spoken for. The one you are holding, Caroline, is not. But, he may not turn out to be show quality. But sometimes it is too early to tell."

"Oh, that's OK. I'm not showing my dog. I just want my puppy to be my pet, ya know, my friend."

"Well, that should work for you then."

"Mom, I want this one, please?"

Corinne turns to Claudia and asks, "How much are they?"

"The show quality ones are two thousand each. The non-show quality ones are fifteen hundred."

It takes a moment for Corinne to catch her breath. She wasn't expecting what she had just heard. Her immediate response is, "Oh my Lord!!"

"Well, they are the offspring of the Number One Show Golden in the country. Some breeders actually get a lot more."

Corinne, not wanting to disappoint Caroline tells Claudia, "OK then, we'll take him."

Corinne and Caroline are riding back to Staten Island, the puppy safely tucked, sleeping in Caroline's arms.

"Honey, I wrote Claudia a check. Do not EVER tell your father how much we paid for him. He would kill me. I had some extra money that I've saved up, so I can cover it....remember, just don't tell him."

"But mommy, he'd understand. He's the son of the Number One Golden."

"Oh honey, Do you really think he would care anything about that? Please!! You have a name picked out?"

"Yup!"

"Well??"

"Dusty!"

"Why Dusty??"

"This'll sound crazy Mom, but when I picked him up, I looked out at Ms. Claudia's backyard and the wind picked up a small cloud of dust. The puppy almost seemed to look that way too, almost like it was a calling of some type. It made me think that I wanted to remember that moment when I found him; the first thing that came to my mind was the cloud of dust."

"Makes sense to me, honey."

Over the next several days, Caroline spends a lot of time reading her book on Golden Retrievers. There is a large section in it regarding training. She uses the tips that the book has to share and spends any spare time she has training Dusty. She takes Dusty to the park daily for his exercise and when at home in bed, he is curled up in bed at her side. Caroline is "on top of the world" as she teaches him the basic commands and watches as he plays with his large assortment of toys. Her Golden Retriever has sparked a new life into Caroline, something that she has never experienced before, one she had never imagined could be so sweet.

Chapter Nine

In Chicago, Curtis is in his kitchen preparing an evening snack and pouring a glass of red wine. He moves into the family room where he puts a CD into the CD changer. The sound of the voice of Peter Cetera, with the band Chicago, enters the room. The phone rings and Curtis, without checking "Caller ID" picks it up.

"Hello, this is Curtis."

The immediate response that Curtis hears is, "I'm not sure if I have the right number but I'm looking for a sexy dog handler guy."

"Yah, you're right, you have the wrong number."

"Oh really??!!....Just when you thought it was safe....she's baaaaaaacccccckkkkk."

"How was the trip, bratface?"

"Well, if you were to meet me for a drink, I'd tell you about the entire trip."

"Well, I'd love to see you Cyndi, but I just got home, had a snack, and poured a glass of wine."

"Did you empty the bottle?"

"Not yet."

"Want help??"

"Aren't you tired, Cyndi?"

"Are you blowing me off, Curtis?"

"Uh, no, no....I'm not. Not at all. I'm just trying to be courteous, you know, you had that long trip."

"Curtis, the Courteous."

Curtis immediately finds himself murmuring, "Well that's one Margaret never called me."

"What was that, Curtis?"

"Oh, nothing. Nothing at all.. I think I was talking to myself."

"Well??"

"Well, what?"

"Curtis!!!!!! Wake up!! I want to see you!"

"No, I mean yes...come over, yes, please come over. I have some food leftover. You can eat it."

"See you in thirty minutes......OK?"

"OK."

"Oh, and Curtis. Don't forget I work for an airline. Thirty minutes means thirty minutes."

"OK Cyndi, Right....see you soon." Curtis hangs up and thinks about Cyndi's "thirty minutes means thirty minutes", and thinks aloud, "yah unless there is weather, or all of the baggage isn't loaded, or the gate is full, or there is an equipment problem, or if the crew is late, or there is a late connecting flight, or if the captain has a case of hiccups, or the caterers haven't finished, yadeyadeyade."

Thirty minutes later to the minute the doorbell buzzes. Curtis opens the door and there stands Cyndi. They greet one another with a big hug.

"Wow, impressive. Thirty minutes almost to the second."

"Well actually, I cannot tell a lie. I was here two minutes early, so I stood outside your door for those two minutes so that I could pull up to the gate right on time."

"Okay, a big 'wow' on that then; come on in and let me pour you a glass of wine."

"Got a beer? My heart and cholesterol are good now."

This little quip brings a chuckle to Curtis. "Yes, I have a few kinds and they're not lukewarm like the ones on the airplane."

"Oucharooni! Surprise me! Hey, what's that music playing?"

"It's an old Chicago Greatest Hits CD. It's the end. I put it on when you called me."

Curtis gets up, grabs Cyndi a beer and changes the music. The next song they hear is the

BeeGees singing "Holiday".

"Oh my God!!! It's the BeeGees."

"Good call. Actually this is a CD of all of their old, old hits, mostly ballads. They were beautiful songs. I love the harmonies. *'It's something I thinks worthwhile if the puppet makes you smile.'* This one is one of my favorites."

"They're awesome and they sustained themselves over all the years."

"Not sure they could have done that if they hadn't been brothers." The song "Words" comes on, a beautiful ballad.

Cyndi winks at Curtis, slides over alongside him and asks, "Wanna dance?"

Without hesitation, Curtis replies, "Sure."

Cyndi and Curtis get up off the sofa and slow dance to the music. They dance around Curtis' family room, looking one another in the eyes, and become closer with each measure. *"It's only words, and words are all I have to take your heart away."*

The combination of wine, sweet tunes, and being alone with "her man" prompts Cyndi to whisper in Curtis's ear, "I'm awfully tired, I need some rest. What about you?"

"Uhmmmm, sure, I could use some rest."

The abundance of intimacy takes Curtis a little bit by surprise but there is no way that he is going to complain. He had taken an immediate liking to Cyndi and he could tell that she revered that which they had up to the time of the "mattress roll". He had thought about her the total time she was gone but he wasn't prepared to "show his cards" sooner than later. He was afraid that she wouldn't take kindly to early signs of aggression or any other indicators of his earliest inner passion. He was glad that she had taken the lead and hoped that the element of lust that drew them together would ultimately be transposed into a relationship on a higher level.

But Curtis did feel compelled to jest with her, "I thought you needed some rest."

Cyndi giggles at this remark and adds, "Eventually. I don't have to get up in the morning and Jimmy has Lucy."

"I appreciate someone that plans ahead, Cyndi."

The next morning both Cyndi and Curtis awaken together. Cyndi is wrapped around Curtis, arms fully extended around his body. Curtis lifts his head from the pillow, looks to the left in order to get a peek at the clock.

"Oh, 'shitorska', Cyndi, I have to go to work."

"Call in sick."

"I'm the one they call, silly."

"So, it makes it that much easier then."

"You have all the answers young lady, don't you?"

With a giggle, "Yah!"

"Well, I guess I could be a little late. Ready for round four?"

"Of a ten round bout?"

"No, four."

"Oh, and I'M the brat Curtis??? Do you have a scoreboard somewhere in this room?"

An hour, or possibly more than that later, Curtis walks into the office, notably late. His employees are jibing because he is uncharacteristically late. He hears a "Good morning, Curtis", almost in unison. The word "morning" is emphasized at a higher pitch. Curtis has a "shit-eating grin" on his face. It became a normal, close to routine work day for Curtis, but he was eager to have the day end. He and Cyndi planned to meet again after work at a local restaurant/bar near Curtis's office for dinner and a drink.

"So, what did you do all day, my dear?"

"Well, when I wasn't dwelling on you, I was taking Lucy to get bathed, walking her in the park, doing laundry, ironing, making myself some lunch, reading, and resting. A triathlon athlete wore me out last night."

"Triathlon? Hardly."

"May I be so bold to ask if you have any plans this weekend Curtis? I'd like to make dinner for you."

"I'd love that but I'm showing some dogs this weekend."

"Around here? May I watch?"

"Well, actually, no. It's in Florida. Orlando actually. I fly out Friday night. I'll be there all day Saturday and Sunday. Two shows, one location. I have some clients there."

"Mind if I go? I can fly standby. I can actually fly to Tampa, which is easy to fly to, and then drive over to Orlando."

"Uhmmm, I don't know, Cyndi. Please don't take this the wrong way, but isn't this going a bit fast?"

"Fast? Curtis, fast? We have had some fun together, had some intimate moments, and I'm asking you if I can watch you handle dogs in a show and you're telling me its' going too fast? What if the show was in Chicago? Would you have objected then?"

"Ouch! I'm not objecting, Cyndi. I just thought that it would be inconveniencing you to fly all the way to Florida to watch me handle a couple of dogs."

"So, let me see if I've got this right. You think I want to go to the show merely to watch you parading around with a few dogs…right?"

"Well, maybe it's deeper than that, Cyndi. I am not sure I've ever had anyone this interested in me. Maybe I am merely shying away from it."

"Well buster, maybe it's time for you to understand that there might be someone out there who really cares and thinks you're a real nice guy, and enjoys being around you. Is that so hard? Shit Curtis, I haven't asked you to marry me, have I?"

"You gonna?"

"You're a shit, you are."

Curtis flies to Orlando alone. He intends to meet Cyndi out there sometime after his arrival. He is at the Orlando International Airport and almost immediately after disembarking, he walks through the airport seeing several images of Mickey Mouse and an assortment of other Disney characters by storefronts as he passes. Early on Saturday morning, he is at the dog show grounds talking to a few different people. He breaks away from the group and heads over to the ring where Standard Poodles are about to be shown. He watches as the Puppies, Open dogs, and Open bitches are shown. It is just about his turn to go into the ring with the "Specials", the existing champions. Curtis hears a familiar chant.

"Yoo Hoo!!"

"Wow, Cyndi, you made it!!"

"Barely."

"What happened?"

"The plane to Tampa was full, so I ran over to the gates for Orlando and I got the next to last seat. Then it was delayed about 45 minutes leaving."

"I distinctly remember you telling me, and I quote, 'I work for an airline. Thirty minutes means thirty minutes'."

"Yah, uhmmm, right, I did say that, didn't I?"

"Hey Cyn, I've got to get into the ring now…See you in a few."

The judge, a man in his early 60's goes through all of the machinations a judge would normally go through in looking at the dogs. He studies them, moves them around, and focuses on each one very carefully. Curtis, employing his magical techniques of showmanship, seems very serious and confident. His dog is extremely attentive and regal looking. In the end, the judge moves Curtis to the front and eventually points his finger at Curtis and his dog as "Best in Breed".

"Wow, you won!!! That was amazing."

"That's why they pay me the 'big' bucks."

"I saw what you did. That was like...un-believable."

"What was unbelievable?"

"Curtis, all of those other handlers out there had leashes, and were tugging, pulling on their dogs legs, backsides, heads, everything. Your dog just did what you told it to do."

"Well, that's the way I train them. I actually get paid quite well for doing that. It takes time though. I have to take this dog into the group competition and I have a German Shepherd to show this afternoon. If I'm lucky, there's a Best in Show competition at the end of the day. Gonna stick around?"

"Nah, thought I'd run over to Disney World right quick to catch a ride on 'Space Mountain' and have my insides turned upside down."

"Gee, you're such a brat. Let's grab some lunch."

Curtis and Cyndi sit on a bench eating some sandwiches and sharing a Coke.

"Curtis, how long do you think you'll be doing this?"

"Not sure, it's a passion of mine. I just love being around the dogs, and the notoriety isn't horrible. I'm not wild about the competition all of the time. There are some politics involved. I refuse to get hung up in that. But others do. It hurts the business of dog showing."

"Well, I was thinking about the competition thing myself. I am not sure I want to compete with all of this for you."

"Well Cyndi, I can't imagine I would be doing this for the rest of my life, but, at the same time, I can't imagine not doing it. It's hard to explain, Cyn."

With a very sad expression on her face, Cyndi remarks, "No need to explain. I understand."

"I need to check on the groomer, and I'll need some time with the Shepherd. Care to join me?"

"Ya know what? I think I am going to take a walk, go look around at the other breeds, watch some of that obedience I saw on the way in, and just 'hang'."

"OK then Cyndi, tell you what. Let's get you a program so you can tell where I'll be and when. I'll look for you if you don't find me."

At the end of the day, Cyndi finds the best in show ring and is not surprised to see Curtis in the ring with the German Shepherd. After going through all of the machinations that a judge goes through, Best in Show is awarded to the Welsh Corgi. Cyndi greets Curtis after he returns the Shepherd to its owners. They pat him on the back as he departs.

"We had a crack at it, but the Corgi is a multiple Best in Show winner. There's always tomorrow."

"You go through all of this again tomorrow?"

"Well, yes."

"Mind if I crash with you tonight, Curtis? In my haste to get here, I didn't think to make any lodging reservations."

"I'd be disappointed if you didn't. But, I have something I have to do for dinner. The Schmitz's, the folks that own the German Shepherd, invited me out to dinner tonight. They wouldn't mind at all if you joined us."

"Oh right! To talk dogs? Curtis, I flew down here to see you because I wanted to spend time with you. You aren't accessible at home, so I thought that this would be a good escape for us. You know I love dogs Curtis; that's how I met you, remember? But one dog is my life, and that's Lucy. The dog show world is your life, it's not mine."

"Well, the dinner tonight is obligatory for me. I understand how you feel. But, I wish you would join me. It won't be for long. I'm tired and I am not at all hesitant about telling them that."

"You can count me in, Curtis."

Cyndi and Curtis are sitting around a table in an Orlando restaurant making small talk with a middle-aged and elegant looking couple. The conversation seems lively, but Cyndi does appear to be somewhat impatient and bored. The two couples part ways at the front door of the restaurant and go their separate ways. Cyndi and Curtis return to their hotel. They are lying in bed and having a conversation.

"I hope that I didn't appear rude tonight Curtis, but, to me, we are in the beginning of what appears to me to be a very nice little partnership. I really DO appreciate what you do, Curtis, but you have a job. You work all week, but then you work all weekend too. I don't want to appear selfish about all this, but I want some private time with you."

"I know, I know. Can we go to sleep? I want to think about all of this, OK?"

Cyndi's only response is to reach over and give Curtis a big hug and kiss. "You're special to me Curtis. I don't want to lose you."

"I don't want to lose you either Cyn. Nite."

It's the follow Monday and Curtis is back in Chicago in his office. It is near the end of the day. Marcy is just leaving and he goes back to his computer to enter a few last minute details. The phone rings.

"This is Curtis."

"Bratface here."

"Hey Cyn!"

"Whatchya up to Curtis?"

"Just wrapping up the day."

"Well, I had an idea and I wanted to know what you think. OK?"

"Shoot, my dear."

"Well, I have to fly this week and won't be back until Sunday. But, the following weekend I'll be around. My cousin Sandy is turning forty and her husband is planning a weekend bash at their place. It'll be a party, barbeque, some kind of entertainment, etc. I'd love for you to be my date for it!"

"Damn, Cyn. I'm going to be in Kentucky that weekend, a show in Louisville on Saturday, then in Lexington on Sunday."

Curtis can tell by Cyndi's voice that she is shaken by his response. "Oh, I see. Okay, sorry." There is a long pause and she does not have anything more to say at the moment.

Curtis waits patiently during the pause, and finally, "Cyndi, are you there? Are you OK?"

"No, I'm not OK, Curtis. I had the feeling that you had other plans. I really can't blame you. It's what you do. But honestly, Curtis, I do care so much about you, but I want someone who is willing to make some sacrifices for me. Ya know, I want to be loved, unconditionally. Of course I would never take you from what you love most, but there is such a thing as sharing. You are not able to do that now. But we can't go on thinking that we might possibly have a life together if you have another life besides me, one that is seemingly more important to you. I'm sorry Curtis, I am so so sorry. Please do take care."

The conversation ends with Cyndi gently placing the phone on its pedestal. Curtis hangs up the receiver and drops his face into his hands. He stays that way, pondering for a while. He looks up a phone number and places a call.

"Hello, Marty?" Curtis listens for his friend Marty's response. And, "Yah, it is, it's me, Curtis. How are you doing?" Marty responds as Curtis listens for a while. Then, "Marty, I have a question for you. I hope you can answer me. What do I have to do to become a show judge??"

Curtis decides it is time to head home from the office. He arrives home, greets Nick, the Cat, changes clothes, and heads out the door. He walks up North Michigan Avenue alone heading towards the beachfront of Lake Michigan where he and Cyndi walked when they first met. As he walks, the first song that comes to mind is Vince Gill's "Worlds Apart". The tune and the lyrics run through his mind as he is walking. *"There's nothing quite as lonely as a sky that turns to gray, or a love that just starts dyin' and slowly fades away. You were my best companion, now we lie silent in the dark, why do you and me have to be worlds apart."* Curtis reaches the shore line and sits on the same bench as he and Cyndi sat in when they first visited the beach. He takes a long, pensive look out at Lake Michigan.

Chapter Ten

Staten Island, New York
(Two years later)

Caroline Alonzo, now 16, has Dusty trained to do just about anything she wants him to do. She is sitting at her bedroom desk doing homework and Dusty is firmly implanted at her side. She puts up her books and heads downstairs for dinner. Dusty rises almost simultaneously with Caroline and rumbles down the stairs directly behind her.

Sitting around the dinner table, Corinne decides to open a conversation. "Tommy, tomorrow is Saturday. We haven't done anything as a family in months. I was thinking I would pack a picnic and we'd take a ride out to the country, all of us."

"The country!!?? What friggin country? This is New York, babe."

"For crying out loud, Tommy, if you are willing to travel a little, you'll find there are some beautiful places to go out in Jersey, or Pennsylvania, or Upstate New York, away from New York City. Don't be so stubborn. That's what families do. They go out and do things together. Do I complain when you get together with your 'so called' group of cronies? I'll answer that one for ya..No! So, don't fight me on this one. Get it?"

"Yeah, yeah, okay, whatever."

Caroline seems to be highly in favor of the idea and asks, "Can Dusty go too?"

Corinne obliges, "Sure honey."

But, Tommy has a different idea. "No dogs. I don't want that friggin hair all over the car. In fact, I wanted to talk to youse two about something. I made a decision about the dog. He's gotta go."

Caroline's mouth drops wide open as she is both surprised and horrified by the unexpected outburst from her father, "WHAT!!!!????"

"You heard what I said. It's gotta go. Every friggin day I put on a suit, it's covered with dog hair. I don't wear them cheapo suits either. These are two thousand dollar Armani's were talkin' about here. There's hair everywhere; It's in my closet, on my clothes, on the sofa, in my freaking' soup for God's sake. So, here's the decision I made; The dog goes or I go."

A deafening silence is heard (not heard) around the dinner table.

Finally, Caroline decides that she won't be intimidated or threatened, "We're gonna miss you, Dad."

The following day, the Alonzos, including Dusty, are riding out through New Jersey on Interstate 78 towards Pennsylvania. They get off at an exit at which a sign indicates that there is a park and picnic grounds nearby. As they get closer to the park, they spot a big tent and several people milling about with dogs.

"Dad, Dad, pull over. I want to see what's going on there."

"You can see it from here. It's a bunch of people running around with them dogs there."

Corinne looks curiously in the same direction and says, "Just pull over Tommy. I'm curious too."

Tommy pulls into the park and they all leave the car. Dusty is on the end of a leash. The Alonzo's head towards the entrance and they see a sign that says "Hunterdon County Kennel Club Fun Match". They walk up to the entrance where they are greeted by a woman in her early 40's with a badge on. It reads, "Hello, my name is Tina".

Tina greets the Alonzos, "Hello, welcome to our fun match. That'll be two dollars each. Are you here to show your dog? There's a five dollar entrance fee for the dog."

Caroline is quick to respond, "Oh, no. He's not a show dog. He's just my pet. We just came to look."

"Well miss, he's a gorgeous Golden Retriever. You should show him today."

"Well, I don't know how to do that."

"It's not hard. We can enter him into the Novice class. Just watch what the other handlers are doing and follow course. You can do it. Plus, you have a beautiful animal there. He'd have fun too."

Tommy is standing to the side just rolling his eyes. "Hey, I thought we were going to picnic. What happened to that?"

Tina is eager to have Caroline show Dusty and tells Tommy, "Oh you'll have time to have a picnic. The novice's don't start for another hour and a half and there's a picnic ground right behind the large tent behind me."

Caroline begins to embrace the idea of showing Dusty and adds, "OK, we'll try it."

One and a half hours later, with Dusty on the end of a leash, Caroline reports to the novice ring. The judge, a male in his sixties, wearing plaid pants, a blue sports jacket, a beige shirt, and a blue and white bowtie, is sorting out the entries.

Tommy strolls proudly up to the ring and asks the judge, "Hey, how long is this gonna take there, judge?"

Corinne, right at his heels has heard enough. "Tommy!! For once, can you have some compassion for what others want to do and stop being so impatient!! This is our day; give it a break, OK??!!"

"Look at all them dogs in there, babe. She's never done this. I don't want my little girl getting her feelings hurt cause there's all those people out there that knows what they're doing."

Corinne's impatience with Tommy is beginning to exceed his general state of impatience. "Can you just relax for a few minutes? This is for novices. Ya know what that means?"

"I know, I know."

Caroline, in an effort to cool her Dad's remarks, "Daddy, I'm fine. Dusty and I are doing this just for fun. I don't care if I win or lose. Like Cyndi Lauper said, 'Girls just want to have fun'. And sometimes dogs do too."

The judge lines up the dogs. Caroline takes Dusty near the back of the line so that she can see what the others are doing and what the judge expects. She figures it will give her more time to get him ready for his turn. The judge reaches Dusty and as soon as Dusty sees him coming, the tail begins to swish dramatically back and forth. When the judge reaches his side, Dusty leaps up and gives the judge a big dog hug. Fortunately, the traditional leg-humping is temporarily withheld.

The judge wears a half-annoyed look on his face and asks that Caroline do the proper thing. "Miss, can you put your dog in a 'stand' position?"

"I think so. Let me try."

Caroline struggles to get Dusty to put his two legs forward and hold his tail out straight. Dusty won't hear any of this and is just his playful self. Caroline's tolerance is waning and she is embarrassed.

The judge, now with a look of understanding and with half a smile says, "It's OK, he's' young and this IS the novice class. Thank you."

The judge moves on to the next contestant. After looking at all of the dogs, the judge hands out four ribbons for 1st through 4th. Caroline is delightfully surprised when the judge hands her a 4th place ribbon.

The judge stops for a moment as he hands Caroline the ribbon. He now wears a much larger smile and "glad hands" Caroline after awarding her the ribbon. "Miss, I'm giving you this ribbon for a few reasons. First, you were courageous to enter the ring with an untrained dog. Secondly, he's one of the prettier Goldens I've seen, so he deserves something. You might think about taking handling lessons. They offer them at some of the larger pet shops or through the local kennel clubs. Good luck to you... and to your dog, of course."

"Thank you, sir."

As Caroline and Dusty leave the ring, they are approached by an older gentleman in his 50's and a young woman.

"Miss, can we talk to you for a minute?"

Caroline hesitates briefly and is unsure as to whether or not she wants to engage in conversation. But, she agrees. "OK."

"I'm Bill McCaid, and this is my daughter Patty. We show dogs for people and we were watching you. We know Golden Retrievers and yours is beautiful, but it was like the blind leading the blind out there."

"I know, but Dusty is not a show dog. He's my pet. We just did that for fun."

"Yeah, but, but miss, and what's your name? He's gorgeous. We could finish him for you."

"I'm Caroline Alonzo. Finish him? What is that?"

"Get his championship."

Corinne and Tommy are now wondering what this conversation might be about, so they inch closer to where Caroline is standing with the two others. Caroline turns her head and watches as her parents approach. She looks back to Bill McCaid. "No, well thanks anyway, but he's just my pet and I don't want him to be a show dog."

"OK, but can we exchange telephone numbers? That way, if you change your mind, you can call us."

"Sure, OK. That sounds okay to me, but I am not sure I would consider this. Mom, do you have a pen?"

Corinne writes their name and telephone number on a piece of paper and hands it to Bill. In turn Bill hands Corinne a business card that has a Golden Retriever on it and the words "McCaid Goldens".

Caroline is curious to know, "Do you breed Goldens?"

Patty, speaking for the first time, "Yes, we do, and my sister and I show them too."

"I see...well thanks, bye."

Bill turns around, waves and also shouts, "See ya!"

The Alonzo's and Dusty return to the car and leave the show grounds.

Corinne is beaming and feels that the day she had planned was a success. "I'm proud of you honey for getting a ribbon out there."

"Mom, I got a ribbon because Dusty is so handsome. I had no idea what I was doing out there. But I'm glad we went. I had fun. Thanks Dad for taking us."

"Yeah, no problem little girl. Glad youse had fun."

Chapter Eleven

Later in the same week, in downtown Manhattan, Marco T., Tommy's "friend", walks down Canal Street, strides through Chinatown, and enters a door in a somewhat decrepit building. He climbs one flight of stairs and arrives at an office door that reads "Thomas L.Alonzo, Accountant". He knocks on the door and upon hearing a greeting to enter, walks in and sits down. Tommy is there to greet him.

Marco is the first to speak. "How ya doin' there, boss?"

"Great, fuggin great! What's goin' on with the numbers biz over on the West Side?"

"It's goin, what??!!"

"No Marco, it's not fuggin' goin'. That's why I asked."

"Whadaya mean, boss? It ain't goin'?"

"Marco, our take is down about twenty five percent from this time last year. We got less biz or else someone is walkin' with our cashola. Ain't you been lookin' at that?"

"People play them New York Lottery numbers and we got some competition out there."

"Hey 'mush for brains', we pay the best odds. Why would they do that? Smart 'investors' don't buy that crap from the competition and the lottery. They don't pay shit! Somehow I think it's bullshit, and somehow I think someone is skimming, and I'm REALLY not good with that. Find out who and get to the bottom of this shit. How can we expect to make a living like this??!!"

"Whadaya gonna do, whack em'? Just a joke, boss."

"No we don't fuggin whack nobody, but there are other ways to let them know we ain't happy."

"I'll work on it boss."

"I got a question for you, Marco. Whadaya know about them there dog shows?"

"What!!?? Nothing. I dunno nothing. There's a big one at the Garden every year. That's all I know. I can't imagine there's any money in it though."

"That's not why I asked, shithead."

"Then why'd you ask, boss?"

"Never mind, never fuggin mind. I was just wondering."

"Yeah, Ok boss. I gotta get outta here. I'll find out what I can find out and I'll call you."

Two days later, the telephone rings at the Alonzo residence. Corinne gets to the phone first.

"Hello?"

"Hello Ms. Alonzo. This is Bill, Bill McCaid. My daughter Patty and I met you at the dog fun match the other day."

"Oh right, yes, Hi."

"Is your daughter around? I forgot her name."

"Well, yes, yes. It's Caroline. Wait just one minute. Caroline!!! Telephone! It's those people from the dog show the other day."

Caroline picks the phone up from another extension. "Hello?"

"Hi Caroline. Do you remember meeting my daughter Patty and me last weekend at the fun match? I'm Bill McCaid."

"Yes, yes. How are you?"

"Fine thanks! We were wondering how Dusty is doing?"

"He's fine."

"There's a regular NKA show in two weeks in Mahwah, New Jersey. Patty would like to show Dusty in that show."

"No, Dusty's not a show dog, sir. As I mentioned, he's my pet. And, he's not trained for that anyway."

"Well, we live just north of there. We could pick him up from you a few days earlier so that Patty can work him, meet you at the show, and give him back to you then. We have a lot of experience with dogs and have a kennel here. The dogs here get better treatment than my wife. Ha ha! Dusty would be in very good hands."

"Can I think about that and get back to you? I don't have your telephone number either."

"Sure, but if you're going to do it, you'll need to call me soon. We need time to get his entry in."

"OK. Give me your telephone number. I'll talk to my Mom and see what she says." The next evening, Caroline phones Bill.

"Bill, this is Caroline. I talked to my Mom and we will let Dusty do this show one time."

"Well, that's great. There's two shows at the same site this weekend. Two different kennel clubs sponsor shows on the same weekend. We'll enter Dusty in both shows. Then, you can meet us there on Sunday and pick him up. How does that sound?"

"Can we go Saturday too?"

"Patty thinks he might be too distracted if he senses you are there the first day. But, we can call you just as soon as he leaves the ring and let you know how he is doing. Can we pick him up on Wednesday before the show? That will only leave two days for Patty to work with him, but she's pretty good."

"OK, it's okay but I am only doing this one time. I don't like it when he isn't at home with me. He's never been away before."

"We'll take extremely good care of him. Give me your address and we'll see you a week from Wednesday."

The following Wednesday, an older model red van pulls up in front of the Alonzo's house. Out steps Bill and Patty. Caroline has Dusty at the end of a leash at the front door. She slowly walks Dusty towards the van. Patty opens the back of the van and gets set to place Dusty into a dog crate.

Caroline seems uncomfortable with the vehicular lodging situation. "Does he have to get into that cage?"

Patty looks over at Caroline and lets her know, "That's how we transport our dogs."

Caroline isn't sure she will accept that as answer. "He loves to ride in the car. Can he sit up front with you?"

Bill acknowledges Caroline's request. "Yeah, sure....C'mon there Dusty."

Dusty voluntarily jumps into the front seat and the van pulls out into the street and leaves. Caroline, looking quite melancholy, stays on the front door stoop watching as the van rolls down the street. The days creep by very slowly for Caroline as she is missing Dusty, terribly. Saturday rolls around and she opts to stay around the house waiting for the phone to ring.

Tommy can see the discomfort that Caroline is trying to work through. "What's going on with your dog there?"

"He's in a show Daddy. I'm waiting for them to call. Since when are you interested in Dusty? You don't even call him by his name. It's 'your dog there'."

"Hey, hey. Yeah, I'm interested. Of course I am. He's nice."

"Yeah sure, he's 'nice', Dad. Remember, he's the dog you wanted us to get rid of because you had hair on your Moroni suit."

"Armani!"

"Armani, farmani, I don't care. He's all I have besides you two, so leave me be, OK?"

"Yeah, OK, OK."

The phone rings. Caroline rushes to answer it. "Hello?"

"It's Bill calling from the show site. Dusty did great. He took second in the Open Dogs class. There were twelve dogs in the ring. The judge really liked him. The dog that won was being handled by a very well-known handler, so he would have been hard to beat. We go in against him again tomorrow."

"Oh, wow! What time tomorrow?"

"Ten o'clock AM. Can you get here by then?"

"I'll talk to Mom. I'll bet we can get there by ten. Thanks so much. Is Dusty OK?"

"Couldn't be better. Patty says 'hi'."

As excited as she could possibly be or sound, Caroline bids bill adieu, "See you Tomorrow. Bye."

Caroline looks about the house for Corinne.

"Mom, Mom!!!!! Mom!!!"

"What honey???"

"Dusty won second prize. We have to be there by ten o'clock tomorrow morning."

Corinne, Caroline and Tommy are at the dog show in Mahwah. They walk around looking for the ring and finally spot Patty, Bill, and Dusty waiting their turn outside the ring. Bill sees them approaching and holds out a hand urging them to wait. It appears that he doesn't want Dusty distracted. Bill walks away from Patty and Dusty and visits with the Alonzos. "It's probably a good idea if Dusty doesn't see you until after the judging. He's liable to be distracted and we want the show to be the only thing on his mind now."

Corinne agrees. "OK, we'll hang back here."

"You're boy finished second yesterday. There were twelve dogs. It's gonna be a bit tougher today. There's fourteen dogs and some well-known handlers in there. But, Patty has him looking pretty good and he's beginning to pay closer attention to her. I'm heading back over. Why don't you stay here and watch from here, OK?"

Bill returns to the show ring and Patty is there with Dusty, comb in hand, doing some last minute grooming.

"Mom, he looks gorgeous."

"I know, honey. They did a nice job with him."

Tommy puts on his cynic hat once again. "All these people making a fuss over dogs. They make a bigger fuss over these here dogs than they do their own kids. They should have a kid show or somethin'."

Corinne feels obligated to stop Tommy in his tracks. "Where do you come up with this crapola, Tommy? We're here to enjoy. If you don't like this, you shoulda stayed home."

"I woulda, but you threatened me."

"That was no threat, Tommy! I asked if you would run a few errands for me if we went by ourselves. That was no threat! It was a request! It was easier for you to sit in a car, so keep your yapper shut, OK?"

"Yeah, Ok, Ok."

The judging begins and Dusty follows Patty into the ring. The judge, a relatively attractive woman in her early 40's, lines everyone up and takes a long hard look. She asks the dogs to go around once and the handlers oblige by running around the ring once. She then lines all of the dogs up again and begins to examine them one by one. Dusty is halfway down the line with Patty.

Tommy has not taken his eyes off of the judge and her mechanics of judging. "Holy shit! She's grabbing the dog's nuts. Maybe I should get in that line. HA!"

"OK Tommy! That's enough! I have no clue why I dragged you along! Believe me, this is the last time!"

The judge carefully goes over each dog. When she reaches Dusty, he holds his regal head erect and stands at a perfect standstill while the judge goes over his body. The judge finishes looking at all of the dogs and asks the handlers to go around the ring once. She then dismisses all but five dogs from the ring. Dusty remains with the five. She lines them up one more time and places them in a different order. Dusty is in the third position. She asks them to go around one last time and points her finger at Patty and Dusty as the winner. Applause is heard and Patty is exuberant. Dusty is jumping around almost sensing that he did something great. A handful, but not all of the handlers, comes to congratulate Patty. A few purposely avoid her. Corinne and Caroline race towards the ring with Tommy following behind. Dusty spots Caroline and leaps into her arms.

Caroline was the first to speak. "THAT was amazing!!!!"

Patty, not wanting to take all of the credit, "He made it easy. I gotta tell ya, you have an amazing dog here."

"Well, thanks! I love him so much!"

Bill, always the diplomat and salesman, "He has the potential to go a long way."

"Well, I know, but he's my baby, and I really don't want him to be away from me. So, the 'long way' he is going right now is back to Staten Island. And, that is where he will be."

"Maybe we can make some kind of arrangement where he only gets shown a little?"

"I don't know. I'd have to think about it."

Corinne lets them know, "We're going to take Dusty home. But, anyway, how much do we owe you?"

Bill, with a big smile, "Nah, you don't owe us anything. If was worthwhile for all of us. Hope to see you again soon."

A few weeks pass and Bill once again calls Caroline.

"Hi Caroline, How's your boy?"

"He's great, thanks."

"Patty and I just learned that there's a show in Eastern Pennsylvania this weekend. You don't have to agree to this, but we already entered Dusty. We had to beat the entry date just in case you agreed. I think it would be a good opportunity for people to see him. This show has some good judges and it draws pretty well. If he won, he could get a major which is a big hurdle towards his championship. Patty and I have confidence that he would be a great 'special'."

"What's a 'special'?"

"Those are dogs that have become champions."

"Well, I have spoken to my Mom about this possible situation earlier and we agreed that this is something we would do, but we have some ideas about how we would want to do it. We want him home during the week, and maybe just let him go out locally on the weekends. And, we don't have very much money to spend, so if it got expensive, I couldn't do it. My Dad isn't all for it and he's the one who pays my allowance."

"I think we can work with you on that, Caroline. Dusty and Patty can make each other a lot more famous than they both are now. So does that mean that we can take him to Pennsylvania?"

"Yes."

"Great! We'll be in touch about picking him up."

Over the next two months, Dusty is in the ring with Patty and at several different shows, all through the northeast. Each time he is entered, he either wins, or he is a close second or third. It is easy to see that Dusty is gaining fame amongst Golden Retrievers, as is Patty, his handler.

Chapter Twelve

Curtis is returning home from work. He stops by his mailbox and picks up the mail. He enters his apartment and is immediately greeted by Nick, the Cat. He is curious about one letter in particular from the National Kennel Association. Before doing anything else, Curtis tears open the letter and reads it. The next thing he does is reaches for the phone and calls his friend.

"Hello, Marty?"

"Yeah, Curtis? How's things in Chicago?"

"Hey, Marty, I need to thank you for your help. Remember when I asked you what I needed to do to become a judge, and you helped me?"

"Yes."

"Well, thanks to you, I've been a judge for a little while now. I guess they like what I am doing because I just received a letter from the NKA and they want me to judge some major shows. I'll be doing some specialties and some of the larger shows around the country."

"Why, that's great, Curtis. Maybe I'll see you at a few."

"Hope so."

"Hey Curtis, what ever happened to that nice woman you met a while back?"

"Oh, right, you mean Cyndi. I blew it Marty, she's gone. I thought I had a special one there, but my lifestyle is too complex for any woman right now. It'll be a while before I can get back on track. Admittedly, I do miss her though."

"You were head over heels with her, right?"

"Yah, thanks for the reminder."

"Maybe you should reach out for her again."

"I tried that a few months back, Marty. I got her answering machine. I left a message the first time, never heard back. The second time, I just hung up. I tried. It's more than over. She was a client of our clinic, but she hasn't been in. She must have decided to take her dog elsewhere after we split up. But, cest' la vie."

"Well, take care, bud. Good luck on the circuit. Glad I could help out."

★   ★   ★

In Huntington, Long Island, New York, Dusty and Patty are leaving the ring after Dusty won his class once again. Corinne and Caroline are at the show since it wasn't a very long trip for them. Shortly after the photo is taken, Patty and Dusty head over to Caroline and Corinne to chat. Bill is at their side.

As Patty beams, "Well, your boy did it again!"

The only words that Caroline can think of to say is, "You're amazing!"

"No, Dusty's amazing."

"Thanks Patty. I guess I'm glad that I decided to do this. But, I don't want to do it for too much longer. I really miss him terribly when he's gone!"

Bill, with a well-prepared presentation tells Caroline, "Well, there's something we wanted to talk to you about."

"Uh huh?"

"The National Specialty for Golden Retrievers is next month. We know who the judge is and he likes Dusty's type. We think he has a chance to win, so we want you to consider taking him."

"Where is it?"

"Well, it's in Anaheim, California."

Corinne feels compelled to immediately jump into the conversation, "California??!! Well, let me think about that...NO!!"

Caroline has some other thoughts about the suggestion. "Mom, that could be fun if you and I went. We could go to Disneyland and Knotts and do lots of stuff."

Bill continues, "I wouldn't be going, but you two and Patty could go together."

Corinne remarks, "That could be expensive."

"Well you ladies don't have to stay in a fancy hotel and they have special airfares from here. I saw that in the newspaper."

"Caroline and I will talk to my husband Tommy about it and let you know."

"Sounds good."

Corinne and Caroline are on the way home in the car with Dusty. "I'm going to address the California thing with your Dad. I'll tell him that you and I want to take a vacation together, just to get away. I am NOT going to tell him about the dog show thing; he'll think we are crazy, which we probably are!"

"Oh Mom, thanks so much!"

Chapter Thirteen

Corinne, Patty, and Caroline disembark from the airplane at LAX airport in Los Angeles. They pick up Dusty from the "over-size" baggage and head for their prearranged rental car. Eventually, they pass a sign on the highway letting them know that they are approaching their hotel. Dusty is sitting in the front passenger seat with Corinne driving. He never stops looking out the window, taking in the sights. They pull up in front of their hotel and are not surprised to see others with Golden Retrievers milling around with their dogs.

Corinne makes the suggestion, "Let's get settled and get something to eat. I'm starved."

"What about Dusty, Mom?"

"He'll be fine in the room by himself, honey. I checked with the Manager. They have made special provisions for security of the dogs while we are here. They expected a large turnout, so they are providing some extra security."

Patty Comments, "My room is next to yours, so you can just pound on the wall when you're ready."

"How about we just knock on the door, Patty?" says Corinne.

The three eat a late lunch and discuss their plans for the show.

Corinne remarks, "OK, it's Wednesday now and the show is all day Friday. Patty, do you have plans for tomorrow?"

"Nope. Just need to get our boy groomed and settled down."

Caroline seems quite anxious, "Mom, can we go to Disneyland Tomorrow? You promised."

"I don't remember promising, but sure, it's close by. Patty, can you join us?"

"Are you kidding? We're in California and I'd give up a chance to go to Disneyland? I think not!"

On Thursday, the three are at Disneyland. Patty, Caroline, and Corinne are taking in rides, throwing their arms up in the air, getting scared in the haunted house, posing with the Disney characters for photos, and finally shopping in the Disneyland stores. At the end of the day, they head back to their hotel where they have assembled for dinner.

"I don't know about you two, but I am still full from all of the junk we ate earlier, plus I'm tired. Patty, what time do we have to be there in the morning?" asks Corinne.

"Judging doesn't start until 11:00, but I'd like to get there about 8:30. Dusty needs to get used to the surroundings then get adjusted to all of the other Goldens. And, I need to do some last minute grooming."

"OK, see you in the morning."

On Friday morning, Corinne, Caroline, Patty and Dusty pull into the show grounds. As usual, Dusty has his head hanging out the window. His tails begins wagging feverishly as he spots a lot of other Goldens with their owners. He seems eager to get out of the car and run around with them. The three pull up to a spot, unload Dusty's crate/grooming table, and head for a shady spot.

Caroline notices, "Oh my God, Mom. Look at all of the beautiful dogs. How can we beat these?"

"I am not sure, honey, but don't forget that we're here to have fun."

Patty, looking very serious at this point says, "I'm going over to the registration tent and get my number. I'll be back in a few. Keep an eye on our boy, OK?" Patty walks over to the registration tent, picks up her number and comes back with some information.

"OK, there are 240 entries in the 'Open Dogs' class, so we have some competition. Many are from the West Coast, but there are several from other parts of the country. We'll just have to try to do our best."

Corinne inquires, "Patty, do you think we have a chance?"

"Never know."

Two hours later, they are at the ring where there are 240 Goldens preparing to be judged. The judge has a small megaphone and asks that the group be split into 4 groups of 60, by arm band number. He will judge each group, and then take the five top dogs from each for the final drawing. Dusty's number falls into the second group.

"I hope the two of you are patient as this could take a while", quips Patty.

Caroline jumps right in, "It won't take that long if he doesn't finish in the top five."

"Oh, he will Caroline, he will."

The first group leaves the ring, and it is Dusty and Patty's turn to be judged. The judge goes through all of the machinations of looking at each dog. In the final minutes of this group's judging, the judge lines up each of the 60 dogs. He eliminates all but 10. Dusty and Patty remain in the ring. As he has them circle around, he points to five dogs. Dusty is one of them. The day drags on and it is now time for the 20 remaining dogs to be shown to determine the best "Open Dog" in the country. The judging of the "specials", the champions are to follow. Corinne and Caroline stand by the side of the ring. As each of the 20 dogs enters, Caroline becomes more anxious.

"Mom, there sure are some gorgeous dogs out there."

"Count me as crazy honey, but look how confident Dusty looks."

The judge lines all of the dogs up as usual and begins his search for the top "Open Class Golden Retriever" in the country. Patty attentively looks the judge in the eyes, noticing that the judge's eyes keep flashing back to Dusty. She and Dusty both begin to get the feeling of confidence about being in the ring with these great dogs. The judge does his rounds and reduces the group to four dogs. He places them in an order with Dusty third in line. As he walks back and forth looking at the dogs, his eyes keep flashing back to Dusty who responds with a "dog smile". The judge sends the dogs around the ring for the last time and points to Dusty as the winner. Screams of joy and applause are heard in the background. Dusty leaps into Patty's arms as, once again, he knows that he accomplished something special. Patty and Dusty get their photos taken and leave the ring where Corinne and Caroline wait, jumping up and down, like little kids. Kisses and hugs are exchanged. They stay for the "Best of Breed" competition. Dusty is entered as the winner of his class, but another dog, well established in the breed, wins. The four head back to the car.

The airplane ride back to the East Coast was smooth and celebratory. Patty remarks that "it was an amazing few days."

Caroline agrees, "That was an understatement."

Patty lets Corinne and Caroline know that the win not only gave Dusty fame, but it gave him three points as a "major" and that he is now only one win away from becoming a champion. It would be one of the fastest finishes ever for a dog, or anyone I've seen anyway.

Corinne, asks, "When will he finish?"

"Not sure. My Dad entered him into the Westchester Classic. That could be it if the judges are fair. It's next weekend."

Caroline wants to know, "Doesn't he get some rest?"

"No rest for the weary."

The following weekend, Dusty is once again in the show ring at the Westchester Classic. This is the show that he needs to win in order to become a champion. Once again, the judge goes through the details of judging and Dusty wins his class. He is entered into the "Best of Breed" competition and wins that also, much to the delight of many of the observers, especially Corinne and Caroline.

Bill, who is also at the show, is beaming. "What do you think of that!!??"

Caroline responds, first, "No words can describe how I feel right now!!"

"Well, now he can compete against other champions. I am sure he'll be well liked and you'll get a lot of offers to breed him", comments Bill.

"Don't be mad at me, but now that Dusty is a champion, I really don't want to show him anymore. I just want him at home." The aura of exhilaration becomes somber as Patty and Bill merely stare at Caroline. "I know that doing what you do, it is hard for you to understand. But, I am so close to Dusty. I just don't want him to be away from me anymore. He is what I look for each day when I get home from school. He is always at my side. When he is away, I am freaking out wanting him to be back. I just can't do it anymore. Please try to understand this."

Bill suggests, "What if we just showed him locally? Would that work for you?"

With a bit more emphasis this time, Caroline proclaims, "No, he's got all the ribbons he needs for now. He's staying home."

Patty, with a heartbroken look about her mentions, "He has a lot of fans. They'll miss him in the ring."

"Not as much as I miss him."

Bill concedes, "We understand, but if you change your mind, you'll let us know, won't you?"

"Sure."

"Oh, and by the way, we can get some breedings for him. He would sire some nice puppies."

"OK, I'll think about that."

Corinne and Caroline are riding home from the Westchester show, Dusty safely sitting in the back seat, just looking around as usual. He dons his "Best of Breed" ribbon which hangs from his collar.

It begins to become dark and starts to rain as they approach home. They pull up in front of the house and begin to get out of the car. Just then, Dusty spots something of interest and bolts towards the street. A dark sedan is heading down the street at a good clip and it is not imaginable that the driver sees Dusty running towards the street.

Caroline screams, "Dusty!!! No!!! Come!!!!!" Corinne and Caroline run after Dusty and are horrified as they hear a thud. As their hearts sink into their stomachs, Dusty lies at the side of the road, motionless with a deep soft whine. The sedan continues down the street, likely not knowing or caring that it just struck a dog.

"MOM!!!!!!!!!! Oh my GOD!!!!!!!!!!!! Do something!!!!!!! Agghhhh!!"

Corinne runs to the car, grabs her purse, fishes for her cell phone and calls 911.

"My dog just got hit...He's in pain. He can't move. Please help!"

"We have a number for emergency pet services. Call 212.555.0070"

"0070!!"

"That's correct, Ma'am."

"Thanks. Caroline, how's he doing?"

Crying loudly, "He can't move Mom, he's dying... Oh no..."

"We're going to save him honey. We have no choice. I am going to back up the car. We'll lift him in."

"Where are we going, Mom?"

"I don't know!! I'll call on the way. We have to lift him carefully. He's bad." Caroline and Corinne lift Dusty into the back seat of the car. He is whining out loud.

Caroline is wailing with tears, "Dusty, please don't die! Stay alive, please, for me! Please! I need you! Mom, he's shaking."

"There's a blanket back there honey, cover him up. Stay back there with him, and hold him."

Corinne dials the number on the cell phone and gets the Staten Island Emergency Pet Care. "I'm bringing in our dog. He's been hit. Where are you?"

A voice answers, "We're at Simmons & 15th Street, on the corner. You can't miss it."

"I know where that is. We'll be right there!!"

"Hurry, Mom!!!"

Corinne and Caroline arrive at the pet hospital. Corinne runs in and gets an attendant while Caroline holds Dusty. Two attendants run out with a stretcher of sorts and carefully load Dusty on it. They carry him into an examination room. Corinne and Caroline follow.

An attendant takes a quick look at Dusty. "He's still alive, but he's hurting. The vet happens to be here. We had another dog hit tonight. He'll be in momentarily."

Corinne and Caroline wait with a motionless, whining Dusty and finally, after 10 minutes, the vet arrives.

"Hello, I'm Dr. Logan. Let's see what we've got here."

Caroline, still hysterical, "He's been hit. Please, save my baby."

"Well, he's breathing OK. He's in a lot of pain though. His whining is a sign of that. This ribbon, when did he get that?"

Corinne answers as Caroline is deaf to anything other than how her dog will be. "Today. He won his championship today."

Dr. Logan, in an effort to comfort Corinne and Caroline, "Let's see if he is the true champion that he may be. Let's see if he has the heart to stay alive. I'm going to start by giving him a little injection here. That'll help with the pain. The first thing we need to do is get him x-rayed. I'll have the attendants take him to X-ray. If you want to go home, we can call you with the results.

Caroline does hear that suggestion, "We're not going anywhere!!"

"Very well then. Why not wait in the waiting room. This could take a while, but I'll give him all of the attention we can. I'll let you know what we find."

Corinne and Caroline wait impatiently, pacing, sobbing. Finally, at 1:00 AM, Dr. Logan appears. He has a stern look on his face.

"I've taken a very close look at him. He is bruised up badly inside. He's young, so I am guessing that he is resilient. I think we can save him. I want to watch for internal bleeding. His right front leg is broken in two places. We cannot treat that here, but we have immobilized him. He'll have a long road to recovery."

Corinne asks, "What should we do?"

"There's not much you can do now. In the morning, we will have a full staff. There are specialists. We will all take a look at him and treat him for the issues that need immediate attention.

Then, you will have to make arrangements to get him to a pet orthopedic clinic. There's an excellent one in Paramus, New Jersey. They are known country-wide."

The only thought that Caroline has in mind at the moment is, "Is he going to live?"

"Well, he's resting now. His vital signs are decent, not great. He looked up at me and I could read in his eyes that he has the desire to 'stick around'. We'll try the best we can to make that happen."

Corinne thanks the doctor, "We'll go home. Can we call you in the morning?"

"Well, I won't be here, but there will be some very good doctors on staff. One will call you in the morning."

"Let's go home, honey. You have school in the morning."

"I am not going to school in the morning."

Corinne is wearing a slight, understand smile, "That's OK honey. I am as eager to hear from them as you are. You can stay home."

The next morning Corinne becomes impatient and calls the emergency animal clinic.

"Hello, this is Corinne Alonzo. My daughter and I brought........"

The receptionist of the other end of the line interrupts, "Dusty, the Golden Retriever with the ribbon."

"Yes. We were wondering...."

Another interruption, "He's doing better but still not up. Dr. James will be calling you in about an hour. They're working on him now."

"OK, thank you. We'll wait."

"What, Mommy?"

"He's doing better, honey. Another vet will be calling us soon. I told Dad about this, and he is feeling pretty bad for you. I know you don't believe he cares, but he does. He told me that he wants you to be happy with Dusty and whatever it costs to get him well, he'll pay for it. He left early this morning for an important meeting, but he'll be home for dinner."

"Thanks, Mom."

An hour passes and the telephone finally rings.

Corinne is the first one to the phone, "Hello?"

"Hi. I'm Doctor Alan James from the animal clinic, calling about Dusty."

"Yes Yes!!??"

"I've got good news and some not so good news. Dusty should recover from the trauma. The good news is that he is limited to some severe bruising, lacerations, and no internal bleeding. His organs all seem to be intact, and he is gaining some energy. We put him on an IV overnight and he responded beautifully. He needs a lot of rest and he should come along. The bad news is that his leg is badly broken and it needs immediate attention."

"What does that entail?"

"Well, we recommend sending him to the Paramus Animal Orthopedic Clinic. They are well known and can get him back up and around again. It would be a long recovery period. He'll need a lot of care. And, I must be fair in warning you that it can get quite costly, but that is your decision."

"How do we get him there, Dr. James?"

"We'll take care of that. We just need your OK."

"Well, you have it."

"We'll make all of the arrangements and will be in touch. We will also tell them what treatments we want to see for him and I will personally monitor his progress."

"When would he be allowed to come home?"

"That all depends on his progress but I expect that if he continues to improve, and he's a strong boy, so he can be home in two weeks."

"The first thing my daughter will ask me is if we can visit him."

"We recommend against it. We want to keep him from getting too excited and to rest. If he sees you, he will want to be playful, assuming he feels better. It might prove counterproductive."

"Thank you, doctor. We'll be patient and will call periodically for an update. Again, thank you for everything. You can't imagine how much we appreciate it."

"Well, Dusty is a special dog. We aren't going to allow him to slip away from you."

"Thank you very much. Bye now."

Corinne hangs up the phone and searches for Patty and Bill's telephone number. She begins to dial. Patty picks up on the other end.

"Hello Patty? This is Corinne. I am afraid I have some very bad news for you......."

Chapter Fourteen

Curtis is driving through the city of Chicago and passes by Wilson's Tavern, the site where he and Cyndi spent their first evening together. It brings back fond memories. The sight of the tavern and the memories it draws upon causes Curtis to pull over and call her from his cellular phone one more time. He was unsuccessful in his previous attempts, but giving up was not a part of Curtis's demeanor. Though he really didn't expect it, Cyndi answers immediately.

"Hello???"

"Cyndi, it's Curtis, remember me?"

"How could I forget you, silly?"

"Well, coincidentally I was just driving past the place where we first met and it brought you to mind. And, not to be patronizing, but you haven't left my mind."

"Well, thank you, Curtis. I think of you often as well."

"I was wondering if we could meet for a beer after work one day this week, Cyndi."

"May I call you tomorrow on that one, Curtis? I have some things going on and I'm not sure of my schedule. But, it would be nice to 'catch up'."

The following day, Curtis is at his desk doing some paperwork when the phone rings.

"This is Curtis."

"It's Cyndi, Curtis. I'm able to see you for a while this evening if you still want to get together."

"Of course I do. Name a place and time and I'll be there."

"How about Wilson's? Seven O'clock?"

"See you then…later."

Curtis arrives early at Wilson's just in case Cyndi is early. By 7:15 he becomes nervous as it is not like Cyndi ever to be late. As his frustration mounts, Cyndi walks through the door and looks around for Curtis until she finally spots him at a table in the back. She holds a finger up as if to say 'wait a minute' and heads over to the unoccupied juke box. She puts some money in the changer, and the next song that comes up as she sits down beside Curtis is 'It's Time', by Boyzone.

"It's so good to see you, Cyndi."

"And you too. How about a hug?"

Curtis stands up and gives Cyndi a big hug. They both sit down and gaze into each other's eyes for a brief while before anyone says anything. Recognizing that some "ice needs to be broken", Cyndi begins speaking.

"So, bring me up to date."

"Much has happened, but not much socially. I'm a judge now and getting some good assignments. Work is fine. I'm attached to that job at the hip and that won't change too soon. I've had other offers but they treat me well and I enjoy the environment."

"Some things never change, Curtis."

"Yah, I know."

"Well, I'm about the same, but I'm afraid I need to tell you something that may not sit well with you."

"I suppose I'm prepared for anything, shoot."

In the background the next song comes on and it's Journey singing, "Don't Stop Believin'".

"Curtis, I think about you all of the time. We didn't work out because you didn't have time for me. I am not blaming you. It's your passion. Well, I wanted to be your passion. It wasn't meant to be. Curtis, I met someone. I met him on a flight on the way back from Tokyo six months ago. He lives in Milwaukee. I don't see him as often as I would like but we do get together frequently and always have a nice time together. I don't want to get into the details, but he seems to care an awful lot about me."

"What's his name?"

"His name is Dave. I don't want to make this any worse for you, so I really don't want to talk much more about it."

"Do you think you'll marry him?"

"I don't know that yet, Curtis. I don't even feel that I know him that well yet. It takes time."

"Can we be friends, Cyndi?"

"Of course."

"And Dave won't mind that?"

"It doesn't matter if Dave minds or not."

Curtis and Cyndi smile, hold hands, and finish their beers. In the background they can hear Elton John singing "Believe". They leave Wilson's and give one another a big hug. Curtis returns to his apartment and hears his telephone ringing as he walks through the door. He picks up the receiver to hear the voice of his sister, Margaret.

"Hi sis!"

Margaret is sobbing, "Curtis, it's Dad......"

★   ★   ★

Curtis, Margaret, their Mom, and several others are standing in a cemetery in Gary, Indiana on a gray, misty day. A minister is standing over the grave site with a bible in hand. He is wearing a long black robe and looks quite serious. His glasses are damp from the mist, so he pulls a small handkerchief from his pocket, wipes the lenses on his glasses and begins.

"Today we celebrate the life of Grayson Edwards. Before I wrote this eulogy, I reflected on the fact that I knew a man who lived his entire life without an enemy. You can likely count on one hand how many people you can say that about. There are several adjectives that I could use to describe him including, but not limited to kind, caring, honest, benevolent, trustworthy, etc. But the simple joy of being in his presence was enough to make anyone honored to say that they knew him. His departure is a major loss and this is a very sad day for all of you here today and the community as well. The Lord will welcome Grayson with open arms and He will save a special place for him above, a place where he can share his life stories with other gracious souls. Grayson will watch us and wish that we too can follow the footsteps that it takes to also achieve that 'special place' in heaven. I invite you to lower your heads and close your eyes in silence for a few minutes. While you do this, dwell on the great memories you had of Grayson and what he may have taught you about life." He pauses for at least a minute. "The Edwards family thanks you for being here today as we lay Grayson to rest. They wish to invite you to the Edwards residence where you can spend time with Grayson's closest loved ones. Let us pray." The minister recites 'The Lord's Prayer', and concludes with 'Amen'.

Back at the Edwards residence, several people are milling around, commiserating. Curtis makes small talk with some relatives and friends of the family. After several minutes, Curtis opens the back door, stands on the back door stoop, and then walks to a corner of the back yard where there is an old wooden cross leaning to one side with the name "Hubcap"on it. Curtis looks down at Hubcap's grave and then squats in a position in front of the cross.

"It's been a long time buddy. You can't imagine how much I miss you. A lot has happened since the last time I was here, Hubcap. It's hard to imagine that a woman hasn't been able to provide me enough to be the soulmate that you were to me. I've learned a lot about relationships because of you, and maybe it has put me in a bad position. I know there is someone out there for me, but who can replace the love that one receives from a dog, especially one like you. You were my best friend. Maybe someday that day will come when someone enters my life and I can feel exhilarated that this is finally the one. Of course I'll bring her here for your approval, buddy. Dad is gone now too. Today the minister said that Dad will be in a 'special place'. I know that it is where you are too, my buddy. I'll be visiting Mom more often now, so I'll be here when you need me. I love you buddy! See ya."

Curtis returns to the house to say his "goodbyes". Curtis, Mother, and Margaret are standing together.

"I'll need to 'hit the road' and get back home. Mom, I'll be here a little more often if I am able."

"Curtis, you say that, but you lead a pretty busy life."

"I know that, Mother, but I may be making some lifestyle adjustments that may change that. Be patient with me, Mother."

Curtis gives Mother a big hug and a kiss and Margaret and Curtis walk out to the front of the house.

"Curtis, Mom is going to need us more than ever now."

"I know I haven't been the best son in the world, Margaret, but that doesn't mean that I don't love her."

"If you love her, Curtis, then show her with your actions. A phone call is nice, but she really needs to see us more often. I'll do my part if you promise to do yours."

"I will try. I will try. Bye Maggot."

"Bye Crude Ass."

Curtis and Margaret embrace and wave goodbye. Curtis heads into his car and heads back to Chicago.

Chapter Fifteen

Dusty and Caroline are in the backyard of their Staten Island home. Dusty is walking slowly alongside Caroline, still bandaged and limping badly. Caroline is helping him through his paces.

"Don't get ahead of me here, Dusty. The doctors say that you have to go very slow. Tomorrow Patty is coming to see you. I'm telling you right now...DO NOT JUMP ON HER! Are you listening?"

Dusty looks up at Caroline as if she said something but he has no idea as to what that might have been. A day passes and Patty pulls up in her van. She is greeted at the front door by Caroline. After exchanging hugs, Dusty hobbles into the room as Patty watches him intently. Patty has a stern look on her face and Dusty, tail wagging, approaches her.

"Oh boy, do we have a lot of work to do!"

"How can you help, Patty? You don't live around the corner."

"Got a spare room?"

"We do, but I'll have to talk to Mom and Dad first."

"And, I'll have to adjust my schedule too."

"Patty, you're not talking about showing him again, are you?"

"Why not??!!"

"Why not??!! First of all, there's no guarantee that he'll ever walk right again, let alone trot around a show ring. And, even more importantly, he's my baby. And, why do I have to continue reminding people of that? This is the last time I will mention it. Patty, he's done in the show ring. Is that why you came here today? To tell me that you want to show him? Well, no! He's done....no more."

"Calm down, Caroline. I came here today to see him, and you. I love this dog. Yes, he has brought me into a limelight that I haven't experienced before, but I've become attached to him. When you told me the news, I cried for three days straight without stopping. I can understand how you feel about not showing him and I can live with that. But, please don't deny me the opportunity to visit with him."

"I'm sorry, Patty. I just don't know how long he'll be around and I want to be with him all of that time."

"It's OK. It's OK. But Caroline, I would like to help you in his rehab. I think I can help to bring him along."

"I'd love that, Patty."

Caroline and Patty retire to the yard where they spend some time with Dusty.

"I had better head home now, Caroline."

"OK, and I'll talk to Mom & Dad about your stay."

"That'd be great...See ya.. bye Dusty."

The next evening Caroline calls Patty to tell her about her parent's decision.

"Hi Patty, It's Caroline."

"I was hoping to hear from you. Did you speak to your parents?"

"I did. Mom wants to know if you like your pasta 'al dente' or on the soft side."

"That's great news. I'll be there late tomorrow afternoon. Who's Al Dente?"

Within three weeks, Patty and Caroline have made great progress with Dusty. He has been "worked" every day and seems to be enjoying all of the attention. Patty had developed a series of exercises for him and each one was carried forth diligently throughout his rehabilitation. He still appears lame but is able to get around and even stand on his hind legs. Patty decides to return home permanently.

"It's time for me to go home. Dusty has done great and it's been a real treat spending time with you family. Your Dad is a kick."

"Yah, my Dad is a riot. I had fun too. Thanks for helping me take care of my baby."

"Don't be mad at me, Caroline, but I have one last request."

"OhhhKay?"

"I'd like to enter Dusty into one last show, and I know what you're thinking, but before you give me another speech, I promise it would be the very last."

"Patty, he's still a bit lame so no judge would ever put him up. And I don't want him to be away from me again."

"Well, first of all, the show is in New York City, just a few miles from here. It's the New York Classic, the largest and most prestigious show in the country, or the world for that matter. And, it's at Madison Square Garden. That's only about thirty minutes away. Caroline, we're not expecting to win. This would be a great chance for Dusty to say 'goodbye', and selfishly, it would give me an opportunity to be noticed. You would have a lot of fun seeing your boy in Madison Square Garden."

"OK, we'll do it."

"Great!!! One last favor. May I come back down here one week before the show to help get him ready?"

"Sure, Mom and Dad won't mind. They enjoyed having you around. And so did Dusty."

"See ya soon, Caroline."

Chapter Sixteen

Cyndi is at home at her apartment with Lucy at her side when her telephone rings.

"Hello, this is Cyndi."

"Cyndi, I'm Diane Lewis. You don't know me, but I found your telephone number on Dave's desk."

"Dave's desk?"

"I know you'll think I am a snoop, but I needed to call you. I would like to visit you if it is OK. I want to talk to you about Dave."

"Is he OK???"

"Oh, trust me, he's fine."

"Then tell me."

"Well, I would prefer to discuss this with you in person."

"Very well then. When can you be here?"

"I live in Milwaukee. I could be in downtown Chicago in three hours."

"That'll work. I need to go downtown to do an errand. I'll meet you in the lobby bar at the Hyatt Hotel at Five O'clock. Does that work for you?"

"That'd be fine. I'll be wearing beige slacks and a light blue pullover sweater."

"I'll look for you then. Bye."

At 5:00PM sharp, Cyndi is sitting, waiting, and finally approached by an attractive, refined looking blonde with beige slacks and a pullover sweater.

"Are you Cyndi?"

"Yes, Diane?"

Diane stretches her hand to Cyndi, "Pleased to meet you. Drink?"

"Sure, Why? Will I need it?"

"Uhmmmm... maybe."

The two women each order a glass of Chardonnay and they are placed in front of them by a willing server. Each takes a sip.

"Cyndi, I'm Dave's wife."

Cyndi is rendered speechless and simply stares into Diane's eyes with a horrendously surprised look on her face.

Diane continues, "Please know that I'm not angry with you, but I am extremely disappointed in him. So disappointed in fact that I will likely file for divorce. It might not have been my business to tell you, but I didn't want to see someone else get hurt as well. He has deceived me and I cannot accept that. Cyndi, I am sure he didn't reveal to you that he is married, with child I might add."

"Oh no........no....no."

"Of course I suspected something was going on as I am quite perceptive about the way he had changed. He inadvertently left your name and number in the corner of his desk with a pile of papers. I really do not like to pry into my husband's personal business, but I needed to know what was going on. I hope you'll understand. I had someone trace your number...I'm sorry about that, so I knew that you must be the one he was seeing. The long and the short of it is that I am done with him. To me, this is damage that is irreparable. I came here to tell you this so that you wouldn't find out the hard way.

I have no issue with you, Cyndi, so as far as I am concerned, he's all yours."

"You're joking, right Diane?"

"Why would I joke about something as serious as this?"

"No, that's not what I meant. You're joking to think I would take him in after he deceived me too?"

"That's your choice, Cyndi."

"Oh, trust me, there's no choice, Diane. If he did it to you, he would do it to me too. Cyndi begins to weep. "I am so sorry. Oh.....I'm sorry."

"You didn't know. I can't have harsh feelings towards you. I just didn't want you to be a victim also."

Cyndi reaches into her purse and pulls out a clean tissue. Through her sniffles and sobbing, Cyndi advises Diane, "Well, for the record. I will never see him again. I need to go. I'm sorry. Call me if you ever need to Diane, but rest certain, he will never see my face again if I can help it."

"Bye Cyndi...good luck."

That very same night, Cyndi is at home and receives a call from Dave.

"Hey Cyndi."

In her sweetest voice, "Oh, Hi Dave!"

"I was thinking that I might take a ride down to Chicago tomorrow and take you out to lunch at the restaurant of your choice."

"Oh really, Dave??? That's so sweet. Which restaurant did you have in mind?"

"Well, I know you love Ricardo's down on Chestnut Street. How about that, sweetheart?"

"Sounds great, Dave. What time?"

"How's one o'clock, honey?"

"OK Dave, that'll work. Just in case you get there a little before me, here's what you might want to do once you arrive there. Tell the Maître D that you want a quiet little intimate table for us in the corner. You know the one we have sat at before. You can get started by ordering our favorite little appetizer, that 'house special' they have there. Then you can proceed to stuff it up your ass." This comment is followed by Cyndi abruptly slamming the phone back onto its receiver.

★ ★ ★

Curtis is returning to his apartment from work. He stops by the mailbox and sorts through his mail. Included is a letter from the National Kennel Association. He saunters up to his apartment and sets the mail down.

"Hey, ole' Nick. Miss me today?" Nick, the Cat responds with a "meow" from somewhere in the immediate background. Curtis walks over to his music system and puts on some music. The Moody Blues' "Tuesday Afternoon" is now playing. He opens the refrigerator and pulls out a beer. After twisting the top off, he takes a slug, sets it down and tears open the letter from the National Kennel Association. After reading it, he sets it down, and picks up the phone, and dials his friend, Marty.

"Hey Marty, it's Curtis." They exchange a few pleasantries. "I just received a letter in the mail from the NKA. May I read it to you?" Marty responds positively. "OK, good, here goes: 'Dear Mr. Edwards, on behalf of the National Kennel Association, we are proud to advise you that you have been selected to judge the Terrier Group at the New York Classic Dog Show to be held at Madison Square Garden, New York City, New York on Monday and Tuesday, February 7th and 8th. We are honored to have you participate as one of our elite judges of this classic show. You will be receiving a follow up letter...ladidadidadi'....." Curtis waits for Marty's response which appears to be quite favorable. "Thanks so much, Marty. You helped me get there, and I appreciate it. Let's catch up later. Bye."

Chapter Seventeen

A month passes and Patty is working on Dusty in the grooming area of the New York Classic Dog Show at Madison Square Garden, New York City. There are many handlers and owners milling about. Corinne and Caroline are there with Patty.

Corinne asks Patty, "Do you think he has a chance?"

"Not sure. All of the dogs here are top winners from all over the country. Some of them have multiple 'Best in Shows'. Plus, I really don't know these judges. Some of them come from other parts of the country also, or the world for that matter. Let's just be happy we're here. This is for fun, and fun we will have."

Caroline jumps in, "I'm good with that."

It is now Monday afternoon. In the Golden Retriever ring there is a large entry of Goldens. Dusty and Patty are in the ring. The judge, a woman in her mid-50's, goes through all of the paces. Dusty clearly looks like the Dusty of old and seems to carry himself more proudly than any of the others. His tail never stops wagging until the judge approaches him. When the judge gets closer to Dusty, there is a noticeable swelling of the crowd around the ring. The judge does hesitate for a moment almost to acknowledge the mild roar, knowing that she must remain totally neutral and follow her own instincts about the dogs. At the end of the judging, Dusty is in front, the judge points to him, and he has won the "Best of Breed" for Golden Retrievers.

Caroline greets Patty as she exits the ring and is jumping up and down with joy. "Wow!!!!! That was amazing."

"Yah, the boy did well. And it didn't hurt that my Dad had all of his cronies hootin' and hollerin' outside the ring. It'll be different in the Sporting Group competition this afternoon. There's a Gordon Setter in there with twelve 'Best in Shows'. That's twelve more than Dusty has."

"Yeah, but look at the fun he's having. A few months back, I thought I had lost him."

"I'm going to get him ready for the Sporting Group competition, Caroline. He needs some rest from all of this excitement. I'll see you all later."

Later that day, the judging is about to begin for the Terrier Group. Curtis enters the ring to begin the judging. This part of the show is televised, so there are commentators offering dialogue to the television broadcast. There is also an arena announcer who is about to introduce the judging for the Terrier Group.

The arena announcer has a deep, professional arena-style voice and when he speaks one can tell that it is not his first time around. "Ladies and Gentlemen, welcome to Madison Square Garden and the New York Classic Dog Show. At this time, the judging will commence for the Terrier Group. This group will be judged by Mr. Curtis Edwards of Chicago, Illinois. Following are the entries for the Terrier Group: The Airedale, Ch. Hagemont of Locust Hill; the Australian, Ch. Loghan's Alpha Reyna; the

Bedlington, Ch. Morgan's Windy"...........and there were several more.

Two TV announcers are assigned to the show including radio and television personality, Billy Blythe. His partner on the broadcast, Greg Jameson, is a long-time dog show aficionado, and a former dog handler himself. Billy is the first to speak. "Greg, this Terrier Group will prove interesting. There are multiple 'Best in Show' dogs in it."

"You're right, Billy. And this judge, Curtis Edwards, is very keen. He's a relatively young guy who started handling dogs as a youngster. He's a real pro and that's why the NKA selected him to do this Group."

"Greg, has this judge seen any of these dogs before?"

"Yes, Billy. We looked into his experience with this Group and he has already given the Norwich Terrier a few high group placements, including two 'Group Ones'. The Norwich is from the mid-west as is Mr. Edwards."

"So do you expect that the Norwich is the favorite?"

"Not necessarily, Billy. At this show, one never knows. But, I'd have to say that he may be tough to beat. The owners have sunk a lot of money in advertising him and making sure that he has been around the circuit."

"Well Greg, the judging has begun so let's see who takes it."

Curtis sends the dogs around the ring. He looks at each one carefully; he then begins examining them one by one. By the time he is close to finishing, he has five dogs in front of the line. They include the Norwich Terrier, the Scottish Terrier, the Wire Fox Terrier, the Welsh Terrier, and the Airedale Terrier. After examining them all, he sends them around the ring one more time and hands out the Group placements. The Scottish Terrier wins with the Norwich finishing second. The crowd yells and applauds with more energetic cheers coming from one particular section of the arena, obviously the owner and friends.

"Greg, what do you think about that??!!"

"Great dog, great movement. He's got a good background, including the fact that there is a painting of his sire in the White House. The First Lady is a big fan of the Scotty dog. It was a good choice, Billy."

Billy addresses the viewers. "Well folks, we'll be back in just a short while for the judging of the Sporting Group. Please stay tuned in as we continue our coverage of the New York Classic Dog Show."

★   ★   ★

On the same day as the Terrier Group judging, a North American Airways jet approaches O'Hare Airport, Chicago.

The voice of the lead flight attendant begins to bellow through the loud speaker system. "Ladies and gentlemen, the captain has turned on the 'Fasten Seatbelt Sign' indicating that we are in our final stages prior to landing at O'Hare International Airport in Chicago. Please be sure that your seatbelt is securely fastened, your seats are in the upright position, and your carry-on bags are safely stowed under the seat in front of you. We should be landing in Chicago shortly. Thank you." Cyndi returns to her jump seat and picks up a newspaper that has been left behind by a passenger. Though it was a few days old, she turns to the sports section and notices a small article about the New York Classic dog show to be held at Madison Square Garden in New York City. She tears out this bit of information and puts it in her purse. Upon arriving in Chicago, Cyndi leaves the plane, grabs a cab to go home, and enters the apartment. Before she even thinks about calling Jimmy to check on Lucy, she heads to the computer to search the Internet for the New York Classic Dog Show. She finds the link and reads it carefully. Sure enough, there is a list of judges and she sees that Curtis is judging the Terrier Group. She logs off and runs to the phone. She dials the phone number for the National Kennel Association.

"Hello? I'd like to speak to someone who can give me information about the New York Classic Dog Show." The person who answers gives her a little information. "I know that it's going on now, but I have a question." The respondent directs her to someone else at another number.

Cyndi dials another number, presumably someone who knows a lot about the show.

"Hi, my name is Cyndi and I'm calling you about the New York Classic Dog Show."

A show coordinator is on the other end of the line, and sounds as though she is eager to help Cyndi. "How may I help you?"

"Well, I have a question. If someone is judging a Group today, would the judge stay there for the 'Best in Show' Tomorrow?"

"Well, usually they do, especially if they have judged a Group. They are contracted for the entire show, but they are almost always eager to see how their Group selection does in the 'Best in Show' competition. I'd say there is a ninety-nine percent chance that the judge would be here."

"Thanks, that's all I needed to know. Bye." Cyndi hangs up and dials another number.

"Jimmy? Hi bud...hey, I need a huge favor. Can you keep Lucy two more days...pleeeeeease???" Jimmy responds that it would be no problem. "Oh great!!!! Thanks!!! I'm heading to New York first thing in the morning."

Chapter Eighteen

At Madison Square Garden, it is time for the judging of the Sporting Group. The dogs enter the ring one by one as the arena announcer calls out the breed and the names. He finally comes to Dusty. "And the Golden Retriever is, Champion Alonzo's Aubrey Dustan." Billy, the TV announcer comments after hearing Dusty's introduction, "Greg, well here's a dog that would be considered a long shot, but he looks quite nice."

"Right Billy, the press notes on this dog indicate that he definitely does not stack up to the others as far as his credentials are concerned. Plus, he was hit by a car a few months back and he may still be a bit lame."

"And you know, Greg, I'm not sure the handler, Patricia McCaid, is very well known either. She's quite young. But, he did win 'Best of Breed', so he deserves to be here. The Black Cocker Spaniel has had 22 'Best in Shows' and appears to be the one to beat."

"Right Billy, and this judge has already awarded him one of those Best in Shows. If I were a betting man, I'd put my money on the Cocker Spaniel."

"Greg, I think you're right. The Cocker took second place in the Group last year, so he is primed to take it this year. In fact, there's talk about him going 'all the way'. The judging appears to be starting now."

The Sporting Group judge, a gentleman in his early 60's lines up all of the breeds for the group. He decides to realign the group based on his desires and puts all of the Spaniels in front of the line. The Pointers are in the middle and the Retrievers are towards the back. The dogs are sent around the ring in a trot and return to their places. For each dog in the group, there is a cheer from a different section of the arena. When the judge reaches the Black Cocker Spaniel, there is a pointedly loud response from the crowd.

"Greg, this crowd knows their dogs. They likely remember the Cocker from last year."

"Billy, it almost seems like the judge has made a decision. Look how much time he is spending with the Cocker."

The Sporting Group judge continues down the line and merely takes a quick glance at the Pointers and the Retrievers. He gives Dusty a passing glance as he walks by him. Dusty turns his head and looks the judge straight in the eye as if to say "Hey, what about me?" His tail is wagging feverishly. Patty tries to calm him and get his tail to the "straight out" position, but Dusty is determined to get the judge's attention.

"Billy, did you see that? The Golden looks like he is actually asking the judge to get back there and 'check him out'. Hilarious!"

"I'm not sure how much tolerance a judge has for dogs that don't comply with ring protocol."

The judge turns and almost evidences a slight smile. He looks back and takes a closer look at Dusty. Dusty stands as erect and professional as any dog that is being judged.

"Hey, Billy! Did you see that?? The judge actually went back to the Golden."

"Cute!"

The judge turns away from Dusty and can almost be seen chuckling to himself. He continues to review all of the dogs and then, once completed, sends them around the ring again. It comes time for the judge to pick out his preferred group of finalists. He points to four of the Spaniels, the Weimeraner, the German Wirehaired Pointer, and the Flatcoated Retriever. All of the others, including Dusty are dismissed from the ring.

"Well, he's got it down to seven, Greg. The Black Cocker's handler is looking pretty confident right now."

"Hey look, Billy, the judge has his hands up and is pointing to the Golden to reenter the ring. Maybe he had some afterthoughts."

"I think he liked the way he showed, Greg. But, you're right; his handler, Patty McCaid, is bringing him back in."

The judge realigns the group by preference and places Dusty in the back of the line. He asks each one to go around the ring. One by one they go around. It comes Dusty's turn and Dusty goes around, but instead of looking directly forward, Dusty is staring directly into the eyes of the judge the entire time around, as if to say, "You'd better be looking at me, pal".

"Billy, that Golden seems to know how to get the judge's attention."

"A real 'showman'. Win or lose, the dog has some character."

Once again the judge examines each dog. He steps back and dismisses all but the top four from the ring. Dusty is placed in the second spot in the line right behind the Black Cocker. The judge looks at each dog carefully. Patty is determined to keep Dusty's tail from wagging.

"Greg, the judge is heading over to the judge's table and is picking up the ribbons."

"Looks like he has made his choices. The Cocker looks like a shoe-in."

"Folks, he's got the ribbons in hand folks and is heading over to the dogs."

Greg shouts out, "OH MY!!!!! He's given it to the Golden. What an upset! Goodness Gracious! I'll need to catch my breath on this one!"

"HOLY COW, Greg!!!! What a shocker! Look, the handler for the Cocker is clearly upset. He's doing the 'deep, down, and distressed doggie stare' at everyone around him." The crowd cheers loudly as Dusty jumps up on Patty for his embrace.

"Oh my, oh my! Greg, that's the best thing about dog shows. There are a lot of objective reasons why a dog should win, but there are also some subjective reasons, not unlike the charisma this dog has shown in the ring. Good for him!"

"I agree, Billy. Well folks, that's it for judging today. Tune in tomorrow morning for the judging of the remaining groups and be sure to watch tomorrow night when we see a new Champion of the New

York Classic crowned, here, live, at Madison Square Garden. Goodbye for now."

★ ★ ★

The following day, Tuesday Morning, at O'Hare International Airport, Chicago, Cyndi is at the North American Airlines gate for the flight to LaGuardia, New York City. She is attempting to get on to the 9:00 AM flight.

Cyndi approaches the gate agent, "How's the load on this flight? I need to get to New York in a hurry."

"Golly, we're full and there's a crew waitlist for a deadhead seat."

"Geez, how about Newark or JFK?"

The gate attendant responds, "I don't know what's going on in New York, but they're all oversold. Wait...hmmmmm...Hey, there's a two-fifteen PM to LaGuardia, only seventy-five percent sold. I'm certain you'll be able to get on that. There will be no shows for that flight too."

"That'll be tight, but great. I'll do that. Thanks."

Chapter Nineteen

It is Tuesday Morning and Tommy Alonzo is in his downtown Manhattan office fumbling with an assortment of papers and is pressing digits on a small desktop calculator. He picks up the phone and calls Marco.

"Marco, get over here to my office. I got somethin' important. It's a family matter." Tommy listens to Marco's response and adds, "no, you idiot, not THAT family, MY family! Hurry up.. time's a wastin'."

Fifteen minutes later Marco enters Tommy's office.

"Listen up, Marco, and we gotta make this quick. Remember I told you about dog shows?"

"Kinda, but no."

"OK, well anyway...here's what's comin' down. Now listen carefully. Caroline's dog won some group thing or whatever at the New York Dog Show yesterday."

"Hey...that's frickin' groovy boss. How much she win?"

"Just shuddup and listen. She didn't win anything, OK."

"You just told me she won, or he won, or whatever."

"Please, Marco, shuddup and listen. Just because I said she won or he won, it don't mean there is money involved."

"Then if they won, they didn't really win?"

"Idiot, Get the fuck out of here...NOW!"

"OK, OK, they won…I got it boss."

"OK then, if you got it, just shut the fuck up and listen to what I have to say. Tonight there is the Championship. They take all of the dogs that won in the last two days and put them up against each other. I think there are six or seven, OK? The winner is the champion of the whole show, get it?"

"OK, I got it. So what do they win?"

"I'm gonna fuggin kill you."

"Sorry boss!!!"

"Look, you and I are goin' over there to The Garden right now. We're gonna find out who the judge is for this championship tonight. We'll track him or her down and I'm gonna have a nice little cozy chat with him or her or whoever the fuck it is, and Caroline's little doggie is gonna win the championship. Get it?"

"Got it boss. Ready?"

"Okay, let's go. And Marco, don't fuck it up… and don't let Corinne, or especially Caroline, know what I'm up to. This is our business. A little help from behind the scenes is always a good thing. Get it? It's what fathers do for their kids."

"I got it."

Tommy and Marco get out of a cab at the entrance to Madison Square Garden. They go to the window and pay to get into the dog show. They also purchase a show catalogue at the entrance to the arena.

"This is a thick book there, boss. How am I gonna find out who the friggin judge is?"

"Start from the front and just read it fast."

"I don't read that fast, boss."

"Give me the friggin book!!!" Tommy now has the catalogue in hand and begins to thumb through it. "OK, lemme see…OK, yeh, here's a list of the judges in front here. It don't say who's the championship judge."

"Maybe we can ask someone, boss."

"We ain't askin' anyone. Hey…OK…OK…look. Here.. look. Group judges, yes! Best in Show! OK, ready? It's Michael W. Moran. Shit, even got his address. CN.. What the fuck's that?"

"CN? Uhmmm.. maybe Canada, boss?"

"Maybe you're smarter than I am giving you credit for, Marco. OK, we gotta go inside and find out who he is and how we find him."

Tommy and Marco enter the Garden and look around. There are many people milling about here and there. They finally find an official who is wearing an armband. Tommy approaches the official. "Excuse me sir. How do I find Judge Michael Moran?"

"Do you know what he is judging?"

"Yeah, he's judgin' the championship?"

"You mean 'Best in Show'?"

"Yeah, that's it. So, how do I find him?"

"Well, that judging isn't until tonight, so it's likely he's not around. Plus, he's probably holed up somewhere. Those judges keep a low profile until it's their time to judge."

"Yeah, well, see, I'm his brother from Canada there. I came here to watch him do the judging thing. He don't know I'm here. Sorta a surprise, ya know?!"

"Well, yes, OK. I am quite sure that the NKA puts the judges up at the Penn National Hotel across the street. You may find him there."

"OK, thanks there, buddy." Tommy reaches into his pocket and pulls out a twenty dollar bill. "Here's something for your trouble, pal."

"It was no trouble, but thanks, thanks a lot, sir."

"Yeah, no problem."

Tommy and Marco go across the street to the Penn National Hotel. They stop at the reception desk.

"Excuse me, miss. I'm looking for a Michael Moran. He might be staying here."

"Let me check." The registration clerk searches the computer while Tommy and Marco wait.

"Yes, we have a Michael Moran. I can put you through. May I ask who's calling?"

"No, No!! This is a surprise. I'm his brother from Canada there. He don't know I'm here. Just give me his room number."

"Why, I can't do that. It's against hotel policy. But, if you'll step over to that desk next to the concierge, you can call his room by asking for his name."

Marco jumps in with a question for the clerk. "What's he looking like?"

"I thought he was a brother to one of you."

Tommy leans over to Marco and whispers, "Will you keep your fuggin mouth shut!" Tommy answers the desk clerk, "Sorry, ma'am. This here is a local friend of mine. He never met my brother Mikey."

"Very well then. I hope your surprise works out."

Tommy goes over to the desk and picks up the receiver of the house phone. In as dignified a voice as he can muster, "Please ring the room of Mr. Michael

Moran. Thank you." After a few rings, the phone is answered.

"Hello, Mr. Moran?"

"Yes??"

"Yes, Mr. Moran. My name is Arthur Winters and I'm writin' this book about dog show judges. I was wonderin' if you could talk 'which me' for a few minutes there."

"Well, uhm, I'm not sure I want to be a source of information for a book. But, I will tell you this. I am heading down to lunch in a minute or two, and I am happy to say hello. But, honestly, I'm not really too interested in participating in your project, but thanks anyway."

Tommy thinks for a second and responds, "Ok then Mr. Moran. Just thought I'd ask. Me and my editor, we're gonna be in the lobby. We'll look for you."

"I'll be down in a few minutes. I'm wearing gray slacks and a darker gray pullover sweater."

Five minutes later, Michael Moran, a distinguished looking gentleman in his early 60's, emerges from the elevator. He spots Tommy and Marco standing near a pillar. Tommy and Marco, recognizing that the man who just left the elevator must be their man, approach Michael Moran.

Tommy is the first to speak. "Excuse me. Would you be Mr. Moran?"

"Yes, I am."

"Yeah, well, I'm Arthur Winters, the writer, and this here guy is my assistant editor, Joe Goodrow."

"OK, I see."

"Well see, we wanna interview you for a book I am writing about dog shows. Can we sit somewhere?"

"Well, to be honest with you sir, Mr. Winters, I really don't feel very comfortable doing something like that, so I think I'll just pass."

"See there, Mr. Moran, passing ain't a good thing cause I really wanna write this book and you here are the authority on the subject."

"Well, passing is what it's going to have to be, so thank you and goodbye gentlemen. Good luck with your project." Michael Moran heads for the front doors of the hotel and proceeds to walk down the street. Tommy elects to follow him.

Tommy leans over to Marco, "Marco, you stay here and do not leave. I'm gonna follow this guy. I need to get him to understand what we're trying to accomplish here."

"I think he already understands what you're trying to accomplish there, boss."

"Just stay here. Keep busy. I'm gonna follow him before I lose him."

Tommy races for the front door and sees Michael Moran walking down the street, then turning a corner. Tommy is in a quick-paced pursuit. After turning the corner, Michael Moran enters Marconi Restaurant. Tommy waits outside, giving him enough time to settle in and order his meal. After a few minutes, Tommy enters the table and approaches Michael Moran's table.

Michael Moran looks up and winces. He has a look of discomfort on his face. Tommy sits at his table across from him.

Michael Moran looks over at Tommy, "Mr. Winters, what do you want from me?"

"Well, foist of all, my name ain't Winters and I ain't no writer."

"Oh really!!?? Imagine that!! You really had me fooled, sir."

"Yeah, well, here's the story. My name is Alonzo. My daughter has a dog in the championship tonight and it is my duty as her father to make certain she wins."

"Well sir, this conversation ends right now. If you don't leave the table now, I will ask the maitre'd to remove you."

"Yeah, OK, not a good idea Mr. Moran. BUT, does ten thousand dollars keep me at the table?"

"Why would someone want to put up that kind of money for a dog show?"

"Ya wanna know why Mr. Moran? Wanna know? Well, here's why. I love my little girl and she loves her dog there. She don't know that I love her so much, so I want to make her happy. This is my way to see her happy."

"By bribing a judge. How foolish, Mr. Alonzo. She would never know that you did this, and if she did, if she is smart, and I am sure she is, then she would have none of this. The answer, I am afraid is a firm NO!"

"Twenty Thousand."

"It's really worth twenty thousand dollars for you to see her dog win? Which dog is it?"

"Dusty."

"That doesn't help me, Alfonzo."

"It's Alonzo and the dog is a Golden Retriever."

Speaking very quietly, Michael Moran addresses Tommy, "Mr. Alonzo. I have been judging dog shows for many years. My record is unblemished. To be honest, I am getting very close to retirement. In fact, I have considered this to be my last show. My wife is ill, and my retirement isn't so strong. An amount such as that which you proposed would be very helpful to me. My integrity must be upheld, so if we did this, it would have to remain one hundred percent between you and me, and I would need your word that nobody and I repeat, nobody ever learns of this."

"My woid is good."

"Mr. Alonzo, I will be back at my hotel at two-thirty PM. Meet me in the lobby coffee shop at exactly three O'clock. I will have my brief case with me then."

"No, Mr. Moran, get a new briefcase, something cheap. They even sell them on the street here. I will have one too. We'll swap them at the table. That way, nobody notices."

"Oh, and I would prefer if you didn't have your sidekick with you."

"Yeah, no problem there."

Unbeknownst to Tommy, an FBI agent had been assigned to track him. The surveillance has been going on for several weeks. The FBI, though it has "bigger fish to fry", has been very suspicious of Tommy's activities, and though they know he is not a major player in the city racketeering business, they have other motives for reeling him in. The agent had followed Tommy into the restaurant and witnessed the conversation with Mr. Moran. He decided to continue to track Tommy. The agent calls for another agent to join him. Later that afternoon, Tommy awaits Michael Moran in a darker corner of the hotel coffee shop, sitting at a table all alone. He has a briefcase on the floor beside his table. Michael Moran walks in, sets down his briefcase alongside of Tommy's. An FBI agent is sitting at a table not far from where the exchange will take place. The agent's partner is seated near the front door. Tommy and Michael Moran are seen making small talk. They get up and each grabs the other's briefcase. They head for the door where FBI Agent Morales meets them. The other Agent, Davis, approaches and also meets them at the door.

Agent Morales is the first to speak. "Excuse me gentlemen, may I have a brief chat with you?"

Tommy is a bit flustered at this rude interruption. "What?? What?? Who the hell are you?"

"Agent Morales, Federal Bureau of Investigation."

"And I am Agent Davis, also of the Federal Bureau of Investigation"

Michael Moran hangs his head in self-disgust.

Tommy, with a most innocent look upon his face, "So, whaddya want from me?"

Agent Morales isn't going to give Tommy a lot of time to talk. "Why don't you two gentlemen follow us into a room over here and we'll talk."

"Talk about what?"

"Listen, Mr. Alonzo. Why don't you just follow instructions? It'll make it easier on you and us as well. OK?"

The four men go to a room in the hotel where they sit around a small conference table.

Agent Morales, short on patience suggests to either of the two, "Tell me what just transpired in there."

Tommy jumps right in, "Nothin'. Why you askin'?"

Michael Moran, in an effort to protect any element of remaining dignity speaks up. "I will tell you gentlemen. I just accepted a bribe from Mr. Alonzo. I am a judge at the New York Classic Dog Show across the street. I'm terribly sorry."

Agent Davis jumps into the conversation for the first time. "Tommy, Tommy. Don't you know better than that?"

Morales, in almost a prepared speech continues, "Look, Alonzo. We've been tracking you for some time now. We didn't expect to catch you offering a bribe, but guess what chap??!! You committed a Federal offense right before our eyes. So, here's the deal. Listen up and listen very carefully. Alonzo, you are a small time racketeer. You are our bait for some much larger 'family' activity we have been pursuing for some time now. It is now time to play 'Let's Make a Deal'."

"What kinda fuggin deal?"

Agent Davis is annoyed now, "Nice language, pal."

Agent Morales once again continues, "The deal is simple, Alonzo. We let you go and pretend this never happened. This guy gives you your money back and you go home. In return for that little 'parting gift', you give us the names and whereabouts of a few key people. You also tell us how and where they operate."

"Are you crazy? You want me to get friggin killed?"

"Nobody will ever know that you're the one who tipped us off. Got it? Do we have a deal? Or, do we handcuff you and take you in? We've got an official vehicle sitting right outside the front door. It's decision time. Deal or not?"

"You shitheads have a deal, but I better be protected here."

Agent Morales wears a broad smile at this point. "Maybe you'll learn a lesson here. Clean up your act? Show some sign of dignity? Ya think you can pull that off?"

"Yeah, yeah. Can I go now?"

Agent Morales seems to ignore Tommy's question and turns to Michael Moran. "And you sir, I'm afraid we'll have to turn you in to the show authorities."

"There's no need to do that gentleman. I will turn myself in and withdraw from the judging."

Agent Morales feels a bit of empathy for Michael Moran. "Listen sir. You seem like a nice, distinguished person, and I am sure you are embarrassed by all this. I don't know what your motives were for doing this other than that briefcase filled with money, BUT, if I were a betting man, I'd bet that Alonzo here worked you over pretty good. Look, we got what we want out of this. Why don't you withdraw from the judging and go home, you know, 'personal reasons'. Nobody will know the real reason. OK? Some good will come of all this. We'll crack a few heads, Alonzo cleans up his act, and you learn a tough lesson. Sound OK?"

"Yes, that will be fine. I am truly sorry this all happened."

"OK, gentlemen. That'll be all. We will be in touch with you tomorrow, Alonzo. Don't disappear out of sight. Because, if you do, things will become much more complicated for you. Understand? So long now."

Chapter Twenty

It is mid-afternoon Tuesday and the North American Airlines flight to LaGuardia Airport in New York City is now cruising at 36,000 feet. Cyndi is reading a magazine on the flight. The flight seems to be moving along at a normal pace and, as is usual, is uneventful. The captain chimes in on the PA system.

"Ladies and Gentlemen, we are now cruising at thirty-six thousand feet on our way to LaGuardia Airport in New York. Though we continue to expect that we will be on time, we have been informed that there are delays in takeoffs and landings at our destination due to inclement weather in other cities whose flights land at the airport. We will keep you posted."

The only thing that goes through Cyndi's mind is, "Damn!"

★ ★ ★

In the late afternoon on the same day as the "Best in Show" judging, there is a meeting of the Board of Governors for the New York Classic Dog Show. Four members of the Rules Committee of the Board of Governors for the New York Classic Dog Show are sitting around a conference table within the confines of Madison Square Garden. Michael Moran is sitting at one end of the table.

Jake Fulcrum, the Board Chairman and a member of the rules committee, addresses Michael Moran first. "Mr. Moran, thank you for joining us this afternoon. We have a few agenda items this afternoon, but we do know that you asked to meet with us. So, we will hear what you have to share first."

"Yes, thank you. Gentlemen, I am here to tell you that I must withdraw from judging the 'Best in Show' competition this evening. I learned earlier today that I have a personal family issue that I must take care of immediately. I have booked a flight back to Toronto and will leave as soon as this meeting is adjourned."

Jake Fulcrum responds, "We are very sorry to hear that but we cannot stop you from taking care of an important matter. Thank you for allowing us the opportunity to have you here. We will find an appropriate replacement. God Speed."

"Thank you for understanding, gentlemen. It may be out of place for me to make this suggestion, but I do know that the young man from Chicago, Curtis Edwards, is a wonderful judge and has very strong credentials. I have judged at a few shows where he also had assignments. He is of the highest integrity and knows each breed extremely well. It is merely a recommendation."

"Thank you for making the suggestion, Mr. Moran. Have a safe journey home."

Michael Moran leaves the room. The Rules Committee continues.

Clyde Berman, another Committee member adds, "I know of this judge, Curtis Edwards, and he is good. He judged Terriers yesterday. He has been working with dogs from childhood. For the sake of expediency, and so that we can put this matter behind us, I suggest we take a vote."

Jake Fulcrum asks for a vote. "All in favor of having Curtis Edwards judge the 'Best in Show' competition say 'aye'." In unison, all say 'aye'.

Jake continues, "Thank you. I'll let him know. I hope he hasn't returned his tuxedo yet." The other Rules Committee members chuckle at this comment. "We have another issue we need to address now. There was a protest from the owners of the dog that took second place in the Sporting Group, the Black Cocker Spaniel. They had learned, after the judging, that the Golden Retriever had been in an accident a few months back and was terribly lame. They suggested that the dog had a prosthetic device inserted, which, by the rules, modified his gait. The protester claims that dog would not have been able to compete had it not had this procedure."

William Cotton, the third Committee member chimes in, "Doesn't a protest have to come during the competition while in the ring?"

Jake Fulcrum responds. "Generally, yes. But, during the competition, there was no way to know that this was an issue. Today, I took the liberty to call the veterinary office where the Golden was treated. They confirmed that the dog did have a pin placed in his leg when it was broken. The owners of the Black Cocker are powerful people and very large contributors to the sport, as well as the NKA. They know that if we take the Golden Retriever down, there will be no competitor representing the Sporting Group."

The fourth Committee member, Calvin Goldman, asks, "What are you suggesting?"

Jake Fulcrum states, "I am suggesting that we will be opening a bigger can of worms if we keep the Golden in than if we take him out. There will be one less dog competing for 'Best in Show', but we will preclude any further actions if we merely take the Golden Retriever out. So may I hear a vote? All in favor?" Three of the Committee members vote to remove Dusty from the competition. One votes 'nay'.

"Ok, the 'ayes' have it. I will advise all of those concerned. The meeting is adjourned, gentlemen. Thank you for your time."

At five o'clock PM, Tuesday, Madison Square Garden, three hours before the "Best in Show" competition, Patty is with Dusty in the grooming area preparing him for the competition. She is approached by a show official. Patty and the official enter into a conversation. Patty is shaking her head as if to say "no, no". She has a frantic look on her face. The official leaves and she quickly grabs her cellular telephone and presses the digits to make a call.

Patty is visibly shaken and tears are running from her eyes. "Corinne, they pulled Dusty from the show!"

"What!!?? Why?? What happened?? Caroline will be crushed."

"There was a protest. I guess the Cocker was a sore loser. They contend that Dusty had a prosthetic device inserted after the accident. They say it disqualified him."

"Wait there! Just stay where you are. I'll call the vet. We were just leaving home. We'll be there soon!"

★   ★   ★

The North American Airlines flight is now 75 miles from LaGuardia Airport. Cyndi is seated comfortably awaiting final approach to LaGuardia when the captain's voice comes across the loudspeaker.

"Good afternoon ladies and gentlemen. As you can tell, we have begun our descent into New York's LaGuardia Airport. As somewhat expected, there is some traffic backup as a result of some weather in several cities which has affected departing and arrival flights from and to LaGuardia. We've been put in a pattern and will be delayed awhile. I will provide you with updates as I receive them."

"Damn again!!"

Two hours pass and the captain comes back on the loudspeakers.

"Ladies and Gentlemen, we have been cleared for landing. I am truly sorry for the delay. We should be at the gate at seven o'clock PM Eastern Standard Time."

Cyndi disembarks the aircraft, runs through the airport terminal at a hurried gait, steps out in front of the building, and hails a cab. "Driver, Madison Square Garden!!"

"You got it, lady!"

"How long will it take?"

"I dunno lady, there's a lot of traffic out there tonight. They got a dog show or something going on over there too. I just dropped someone there an hour ago."

"I know, I know...That's where I'm going... Hurry, please."

"I'll do the best I can."

Chapter Twenty-one

It is now 7:45 PM at Madison Square Garden and the TV commentators, Billy Blythe and Greg Jameson, are preparing the viewers for the "Best in Show" competition. Billy is the first one to speak.

"Good evening folks and welcome back to Madison Square Garden and the New York Classic Dog Show. Well Greg, it's time for the Best in Show Competition. Any thoughts?"

"There are some great dogs in here, Billy. If there is a favorite, I'm not sure who it might be. Do you have a favorite?"

"I like them all Greg. The Scottish Terrier has a great following and has several Best in Shows under his belt, or collar. But, it's anyone's game. Folks, we are going to take a break, and when we come back, the judging for 'Best in Show' will begin."

★ ★ ★

It is now Eight o'clock PM and Cyndi is just leaving the cab in front of Madison Square Garden. She heads for the doors to the show. At the ticket window, she purchases a standing room only ticket and makes her way into the crowd. With backpack over her shoulder, she finds a spot to stand. From behind the last row of seats on the lower level of the arena, Cyndi can see that she has arrived just in time for the judging. Curtis is standing beside the center ring chatting with what appears to be a show official. Each dons an official looking badge which hangs on a red, white, and blue ribbon around their necks. The sight of Curtis sends a chill through Cyndi.

Billy Blythe is back on the air. "Folks, we're back now. Let's hear from the arena announcer."

"Good evening ladies and gentlemen and welcome to Madison Square Garden for the judging of the 'Best in Show' competition in the ninetieth annual New York Classic Dog Show. We have a few announcements prior to the commencement of the judging. First, Mr. Michael Moran, the 'Best in Show' Judge, has withdrawn from the judging assignment and will be replaced by Mr. Curtis Edwards of Chicago, Illinois." A loud murmur is heard from the crowd. "Also, we regret to advise you that the winner of the Sporting Group, the Golden Retriever, has been disqualified from the competition. There will be only six participants in the Best in Show Competition." Following this statement, a very loud murmur and a few boos are heard from the crowd.

"Billy, Wow!! This is a sudden turn of events. I wonder what happened here. Those are two major announcements in one show, both of which are rare events."

"I don't know, Greg, but it certainly appears that the crowd is not happy with the decision regarding the Golden Retriever."

In the meantime, Dr. Alan James, the veterinarian who saw Dusty after his accident, makes his way through the arena crowd. He is approaching the boxes where the show officials are seated. He is making an effort and seems determined to reach the show officials' box.

The arena announcer continues, "Ladies and gentlemen, here are the dogs representing the six groups for the 'Best in Show' competition. First, representing the Hound Group, the Norwegian Elkhound, Champion Margot's Mountain Jolly." The crowd politely applauds with some voiced cheers coming from a few sections. "Next, representing the Toy Group......" Just then, Bill McCaid, standing with a group of friends, including the Alonzos, begins chanting.....

"Dus-ty, Dus-ty, Dus-ty, Dus-ty,........."

The group surrounding Bill McCaid and the Alonzos also join in the chant, "Dus-ty, Dus-ty, Dus-ty, Dus-ty....." Within just a minute, it seems like the entire arena is chanting Dusty's name. The chant becomes so loud that it drowns out the voice of the arena announcer who is trying to introduce the other Best in Show dogs.

Billy Blythe takes notice, "Folks, you are hearing a very first at this dog show. The crowd is voicing its displeasure about the removal of the Golden Retriever from the competition."

His partner, Greg Jameson, also takes notice. "Well Billy, he won their hearts in the Group competition with his charisma. Plus, many know the history of this dog. He was in a life-threatening accident a few months back. Not only did he barely make it, but he was destined never to be shown again. He's a courageous dog."

The arena announcer pauses and waits for the crowd to quiet down. It appears that it will not happen too soon. The announcer looks towards the officials' box where the show officials are chattering feverishly amongst themselves. Dr. Alan James finally makes it to the box and seems to be fuming.

Dr. James is practically in the faces of the show officials at this point. "Excuse me! Excuse me gentlemen!" All of the officials, each, seemingly with a look of confusion about them, look up at their visitor. "I'm Dr. James from the Staten Island Animal Clinic. I saw the Golden Retriever after the accident and have tracked his progress. What in the HELL is this all about? What prosthetic device? The dog has a pin in his leg. I was one of the first to treat him! I read the rules...they're right here: 'A dog is considered changed in appearance by artificial means if it has been subjected to any type of procedure that has the effect of obscuring, disguising, or eliminating any congenital or hereditary abnormality or any undesirable characteristic, or anything that improves a dog's natural appearance, temperament, bite or gait'. You gentlemen have made a huge mistake here. For crying out loud, this dog had a pin placed in his leg to help save his life!!! He worked hard and courageously to come back to what he loves to do and you're going to deprive him of his 'fifteen minutes of fame'??!! This, gentlemen, is a travesty, and you know it!!! You succumbed to the wishes of some snooty dog owner which is pure sour grapes. And, in case you weren't aware, the rules also say that 'Only exhibitors in the ring have the right to protest dogs. Protests are NOT allowed after every dog in the class has been individually examined and gaited.' If you uphold your decision, you will have violated the Association rules, you will feel the wrath of everyone in this arena tonight, and you will live with this for the remainder of your lives."

Dr. James turns and abruptly walks away from the officials' box. The show officials once again commence discussions amongst themselves.

"Greg, I'm not sure what's going on over there, but there seems to be some serious discussions."

"Folks, we're sorry for the delay, but at this point, we aren't really sure what is happening up there. We will bring you up to speed as soon as we know."

The show officials summons the arena announcer to their box. After a few minutes discussion, the arena announcer is seen nodding his head vertically and returning to his microphone.

"Ladies and gentlemen."The crowd comes to a deafening silence awaiting his word. Curtis looks up in wonderment from beside the ring. All eyes are on the speakers.

"We are sorry for the interruption. The show officials have reviewed the matter of the winner of the Sporting Group. I am pleased to announce that the Sporting Group WILL be represented in the 'Best in Show' competition by the Golden Retriever, Champion Alonzo's Aubrey Dustan."

The crowd cheers loudly as the other 'Best in Show' finalists are introduced. Patty is in the grooming area with Dusty working on packing up her bags and crate when she is told of the news. She asks another handler to watch Dusty as she runs with her dress in hand in order to change. Nearly tripping over herself, she makes it to the women's rest room where she quickly changes. She runs back to the grooming area, grabs a comb and a brush, quickly brushes through Dusty's coat, and hurries to the ring. The crowd cheers loudly, whistles, and applauds when she enters the ring with Dusty. Curtis looks towards her with a stern look on his face.

"Well Greg, this is indeed unprecedented."

"Billy, it's rare that you see almost the entire crowd getting caught up with one dog."

"The Golden is very charismatic, Greg. But, it'll take more than charisma to beat this group of dogs, and to win over this judge. A Golden Retriever has never ever won this show."

"That's right, Billy. And, Curtis Edwards has the reputation for being extremely fair. He is said to know every specific conformation detail from practically every breed."

"Yes Billy, and, that's probably the reason why the show officials moved him into the 'Best in Show' competition."

"Greg, and viewers, it looks like the 'Best in Show' judging is beginning."

One by one, the seven finalists for the 'Best in Show' competition enter the ring. The people in the crowd, each having their own favorite, are whooping, hollering, and whistling for each of the breeds as they enter the ring. Patty looks somewhat tentative, but Dusty appears to be leading her with confidence.

"Greg, these dogs are smart. Each one knows exactly why he or she is in the ring. For them, it's just another day in the office."

"I agree, Billy. Folks, make your picks and we'll be right here with you."

Curtis begins looking at the dogs that are all lined up in front of him. He examines them in no particular order. Dusty and Patty stand firm with Dusty looking straight ahead without looking at the judge in his characteristic manner. Dusty turns to look at Curtis only when Curtis isn't looking directly at him. Curtis, out of the corner of his eye sees Dusty following him with his eyes. But, when he turns back to look at Dusty, Dusty quickly turns his head straight forward.

"Billy, do you see what is happening there? The Golden is playing 'cat & mouse' with the judge. Unbelievable! I can't imagine a dog being trained to do that."

"I didn't notice Greg, but this dog is known to seek what he wants...He's a smart one."

Curtis again goes down the line of the seven dogs and one by one he examines them carefully. Then, again, one by one, he sends them around the ring. Patty and Dusty take their lap around the ring, Dusty never moving his head from the straightforward position. Curtis pretends to turn his head looking in another direction and Dusty quickly looks at him. Curtis catches him in the act and gives Dusty the 'gotchya' look. Curtis finishes the tedious task of examining each dog. Ten minutes later, he asks everyone to stay in their places and walks over to the judge's desk beside the ring. He picks up the Best in Show trophy. Curtis then walks to the center of the ring.

The arena announcer is once again ready to address the crowd. "Ladies and Gentlemen, Judge Curtis Edwards has made his decision. The winner, and 'Best in Show' at the Ninetieth Annual New York Classic Dog Show, is the Golden Retriever, Champion Alonzo's Aubrey Dustan." The crowd roar is a mixture of surprise, amazement, delight, and overall excitement. There are a few dismayed patrons, but the solid majorities are hugely delighted with the choice.

Cyndi begins making her way through the crowd to the stage. Bill McCaid and the Alonzo's head for the ring. The crowd is in a frenzy. Patty and Dusty are in the center of the ring exuberantly embracing as Dusty leaps up to be in Patty's arms.

Billy Blythe, catching his breath says, "This is absolutely amazing folks. For the first time in this show's history, an underdog, excuse the expression, has won and the crowd loves it. Greg, this dog has shown charisma, intelligence, and great beauty, and tonight Curtis Edwards noticed it and made him the Champion."

"Folks, Billy and I are heading down to the ring where the presentation is about to be made."

The arena announcer continues, "We direct your attention to the center of the ring where the presentation for 'Best in Show' is being made."

In the center of the ring stand Dusty, Patty, Curtis, Corinne, and Caroline Alonzo. Curtis stands off to the side as Cyndi continues to make her way down a series of steps and towards the ring. Cyndi finally reaches a guard to the floor and tells the guard that she must be let through.

"I'm sorry, ma'am. Only show officials go through this gate."

"Demonstrably pointing her finger towards Curtis, "Well, I'm sorry too. That's my future husband standing there in the tuxedo. He needs me there and that's where I am going! Please move now. I am going out there, now! Do not try to stop me."

"But ma'am ….. No, stop." Cyndi busts through the gate and rushes towards Curtis. He sees her, embraces her and holds her tight in front of the large crowd.

Board member Jake Fulcrum is now holding the microphone. "Good evening, Ladies and Gentlemen. It is with extreme pleasure that I present the Trophy for 'Best in Show' to Champion Alonzo's Aubrey Dustan." He looks down at Caroline. "Young lady, I understand that this dog belongs to you. On behalf of the great City of New York, the New York Classic Dog Show, and Madison Square Garden, we thank you for bringing such a wonderful dog to our show and wish you only the very best for the future."

Caroline looks up at Jake Fulcrum and quietly asks, "May I say something?"

Jake responds, "Of course you may, young lady."

Caroline now has the microphone in hand. She calmly awaits the crowd to settle down until there is only a slight murmur remaining. "Thank you everybody for falling in love with my boy, Dusty. I am the happiest girl in the world right now. Dusty almost couldn't be here tonight for many reasons, but he knew that he must, so he did it. And, he won." Once again there is a roar from the crowd. She patiently awaits her turn again. "Tonight has been a new beginning for Dusty and me as we have had the chance to 'say hello' to you again after many months. But, also, for now, he will be saying goodbye to all of you. This will be his last show, but he will not stop loving you and I hope that you will not stop loving him. Thank you." Once again, there is a loud roar from the crowd.

Curtis is taking all of this in. He leans over and whispers to Cyndi, "Guess who else is retiring tonight."

"I love you, Curtis."

Patty hands Dusty's leash to Caroline. "Caroline, why don't you take Dusty around the arena?"

Caroline grabs hold of Dusty's leash and begins a trot around the arena. Almost as if they are moving in slow motion, Dusty's beautiful feathers fly through the air as they move. The crowd is on their feet and applauding as they circle the ring. As Caroline's trot around the arena ends, Dusty leaps into her arms.

"this is my last dance,
I'm walking off the floor where I belong….."

Swan Song, Bee Gees, 1968

The End

CPSIA information can be obtained at www.ICGtesting.com
Printed in the USA
BVOW03*1805160315

391907BV00003B/7/P

9 781618 565860